Chocolate Cake and Chaos

A Peridale Cafe
MYSTERY

AGATHA FROST

Other books in the Peridale Café Series

A

Peridale Cafe
MYSTERY

Book Four

CHAPTER 1

"Try this one," Barker said, handing Julia a small sample of dark beer. "I think this is my favourite so far."

Julia looked unsurely at the beer, the taste of the last sample still staining her tongue. She looked back at the long line of barrels, sure each new beer had been Barker's favourite. Julia's taste buds had always been uncertain of beer, but it had taken the first annual Peridale Craft Beer Festival to assure her she was more of a peppermint and liquorice tea kind of woman.

"It's certainly malty," Julia said, wincing after taking a small sip. "I'm not sure I have the tongue for the subtleties this requires."

"You're just not an IPA beer kind of girl," Barker said defiantly, taking the sample from her and placing it back on the table. "There's a drink out there for everyone."

Julia wasn't so sure, but she followed Barker to the next barrel, smiling her apologies to the brewer for not choosing his batch.

"This should be a little smoother." Barker picked up two samples from the small tray sitting in front of the barrel on the next table. "Smells fruity, don't you think?"

"Smells like ale," Julia mumbled as she inhaled the amber liquid. "*Bottoms up!*"

They clinked their plastic shots, and instead of sipping this one, she tossed it back like Barker had been doing, hoping it would affect the taste. She swallowed, wincing as she had with the others. It didn't leave as strong an aftertaste, and it was definitely smoother, but Julia couldn't detect the fruitiness Barker had assured her of. Glancing over her shoulder at the dozen more ales to taste in the white tent outside of The Plough pub, she opted for half a pint of the one she had just tried in hopes it would appease Barker. If he hadn't looked like a kid in a toyshop when he had first heard about the festival coming to Peridale, she would have stayed home and spent her Sunday afternoon de-weeding her daffodil beds.

"I guess you weren't one of those teenagers who drank alcohol on street corners?" Barker asked as they took their drinks to one of the free benches.

"I was more of a stay home and bake girl."

"I should have known," Barker said with a wink. "That's why you're so good at it."

Most of Peridale had turned out for the festival, which had been organised by Shelby and Bob Hopkins, the owners of The Plough. They had been talking about pulling something together for years, but life in Peridale moved slowly, so most people expected it to stay nothing more than just talk. Julia suspected a lot of the visitors were showing their faces to see if there was anything worth gossiping about for the coming week, but so far the event had run a lot smoother than the alcohol Julia was forcing down.

"Here comes trouble," Barker whispered over his pint, nodding towards the opening of the tent.

"*Code Grey.*"

Julia followed his eyeline to a group of senior women, fronted by her gran, Dot. They were decked out in brightly coloured and mismatched tracksuits, with even brighter neon sweatbands pushing their permed curls away from their faces. It reminded Julia of the 1980's workout videotapes her gran had tried and failed to complete when Julia was a little girl.

"I see you're polluting your body with the rest of them, Julia," Dot called out loudly enough for everybody within earshot to hear as she marched over, her knees and elbows lifting dramatically. "It's a beautiful day out. Why don't you put down that poison and join our fitness group?"

Dot continued to march on the spot, squinting at the expensive new exercise watch on her wrist that she had recently purchased. Julia had tried to teach her how to use it correctly, but the technology had gone over her head. She missed the days when devices had buttons and not just touchscreens.

"I think I'll pass today, Gran," Julia said, smiling to the rest of the girls behind Dot, who didn't seem as enthusiastic about their new club. "Clocking up lots of steps?"

"Eight thousand so far this morning," she

announced proudly. "I've decided we should do one hundred steps for every year of our age. Since I appear to be the oldest, we've got another three hundred left."

There was a grumble from the girls as they adjusted their sweatbands and sluggishly attempted to copy Dot's eagerness. It had only been a week since Dot had started her new health-kick club, but Julia was sure the numbers were already dwindling.

"You should take it a little easier," Julia suggested after sipping her beer. "Remember what the doctor said about your tricky hip?"

"My hip has never felt better, thank you very much!" Dot cried. "We've got another lap of the village green before we can sit down. Barker, you should stop eating so many of Julia's cakes. You're starting to get fat. *Must dash.*"

Dot twirled around, pushed through the girls, and power-walked out of the tent, her head held high and her shoulders forced back. The rest of the girls followed, some of them eyeing the barrels of beer longingly as they left.

"Am I getting fat?" Barker mumbled as he prodded the tiny bit of softness poking through his white shirt.

"Ignore her. She saw some documentary about

fitness for old people on the telly, and she hasn't shut up about it since. She's already warned me about the dangers of heart disease four times this week. Sue and I went to her cottage for dinner last night, and she lectured us about meat and dairy while we ate steamed asparagus and kale. Knowing Gran like I do, she will be bored in a couple of days and she'll already be onto the next thing."

"You didn't answer my question."

"Of course you're not getting fat!" Julia insisted with a chuckle. "You're in better shape than most men in this village."

"Only *most* men?"

"Do you want me to tell you you're in the best shape to make you feel better?"

"Yes, please."

"You're in the best shape, Barker," Julia said, glancing down to his barely there stomach. "Although maybe she's right about the cakes."

"That's your fault!" Barker cried, readjusting his posture so he could suck his minuscule stomach in. "You know chocolate cake is my weakness."

"I'm trying to perfect my recipe," she said casually. "Nobody is forcing you to eat it."

"Maybe if you weren't such a great baker, I wouldn't need to. Perhaps you *should* have been that teenager who drank beer on the street corner?"

He winked and kissed her on the cheek, the malty scent of ale lingering on his breath. Julia felt her face flush as the kiss sent the pit of her stomach into a wild swirl. It had been three weeks since they had confessed their love to each other after only a couple of months of dating, but it was the small things that kept taking Julia by surprise. After twelve years of marriage to a man whose idea of romance was buying Julia a bottle of whatever perfume was on sale once a year on Valentine's Day, Julia was enjoying the feeling of being in love.

"Oh, more trouble," Barker mumbled, nodding to the opening of the tent once more.

Julia turned around with his kiss still fresh on her cheek. Her heart skipped another beat when she saw Jessie, her sixteen-year-old lodger, sneaking in, a hood pulled low over her pale face. Leaving her beer, Julia hurried through the crowd and across the tent, her pastel yellow dress fluttering behind her.

"What are *you* doing here?" Jessie demanded, looking down her nose at Julia, her lips snarling into a scowl.

"*I'm* the one who should be asking that."

"You hate beer."

"I'm here with Barker."

"Oh," Jessie said with a roll of her eyes. "I was bored at home. Thought I'd come and see what was happening here."

"And not to try and sneak some underage alcohol?" Julia asked with a smirk as she folded her arms across her chest. "You're right, I don't like beer. Let me grab my bag, and we'll head home."

Jessie grumbled as she slid her hood back to let her dark hair fall over her shoulders. She had been living with Julia and working in her café for four months now. Their relationship had begun with Jessie breaking into Julia's café and stealing cakes because she was homeless, but it had developed into something that resembled mother and daughter. Julia hadn't expected to suddenly have a teenage girl in her life to look after, but it was a challenge she was enjoying. Jessie was a good kid, most of the time.

Leaving Jessie lingering by one of the barrels, Julia headed back to the bench she had been sitting at with Barker. Her half-full plastic cup of beer was still there, along with Barker's now empty cup, but Barker and her bag had disappeared. She spun on the spot and was relieved to see him getting a refill of the IPA that had almost made Julia gag. That relief turned into a steel weight when she didn't see him carrying her handbag.

"Barker! Where's my bag?"

Barker walked back to the bench, his fresh pint crammed firmly against his top lip. After a deep gulp, he set it down and looked under the bench, a little less urgently than Julia would have liked.

"You had a bag?"

"*Men*!" Julia cried, pushing her hands up into her hair as she spun on the spot. "I think somebody has stolen it!"

They both scanned the tent, their eyes landing on the same thing at the same time. A hooded figure in a red tracksuit was hurrying through the tent and towards the opening, clutching Julia's bag under their arm. They gazed at each other, frozen for a moment before they set off at a run. The figure looked over their shoulder, revealing the face of a teenage boy.

"*Stop him*!" Julia cried as she felt the nauseating sinking of despair. "He's stolen my bag!"

The boy began to sprint, but as he approached the entrance to the tent, he slammed into two men who had just walked in. There were gasps from the watching crowd as he was thrown to the ground, dropping the bag as he landed in a heap. But just as Julia breathed a sigh of relief, the nimble teenager scrambled to his feet, grabbing the bag in the process before either of the thick-necked men could figure out what was happening.

Side by side, Julia and Barker burst out of the tent, the bright May sunshine blinding them. They stood outside of The Plough, looking up and down the crowded village street.

"*There*!" Barker cried before setting off at a sprint. "He's heading towards the village green!"

Julia kicked off her kitten heels, hitched up her dress, and set off running, catching up with Barker in seconds, her tights-covered feet pounding into the cobbled road. She didn't care about her phone, or even her café's takings that were in her bag from the busy Saturday shift the night before, but she did care about her small notepad, which had all of her recipe revisions and notes for the chocolate cake she was working on.

The boy's hood flew down as he darted across the village green. Dot and her speed walking group all stopped to gawp at the commotion.

"Stop that boy!" Barker cried through bated breath. "*Stop* him!"

The women all looked to one another as they fumbled from side to side, none of them appearing to know what to do. Dot, on the other hand, charged at the boy, seemingly forgetting the existence of her eighty-three-year-old tricky hip once again. The boy smirked over his shoulder, eyes wide as Peridale's finest came at him from both directions.

"*Stop!*" Dot cried, letting out a tribal scream as her Day-Glo green sweatband flew off, unleashing her recently permed curls. "*Thief!*"

Like a rugby player going for a below the belt tackle, Dot dove in, but like an even better player, the boy darted out of her way. She fell into the neatly mowed grass and rolled over onto her side. Julia gave up on her recipe notepad and ran to her gran's aid.

"I *almost* had him!" Dot said through shallow breaths. "I was – I was *so* close."

"It doesn't matter," Julia said, crouching down to her gran. "I'm calling an ambulance."

"You'll do no such thing!" Dot cried as she stumbled up to her feet, instantly checking her watch. "I've just finished my steps for the day. And a new calorie-burning record to boot! Ladies, another lap around the green for you!"

As though nothing had happened, Dot scooped up her sweatband, reapplied it, and marched back to her group. Julia turned her attention back to the boy, who was sprinting full force towards St. Peter's

Church with Barker lagging behind. Resting a hand on her forehead, she wanted to cry out to tell Barker to leave it, but at that moment, a black blur darted in front of the boy, knocking him clean off his feet as he entered the church grounds. The figure flicked their dark hair back, and Julia was startled when she saw that it was Jessie who was pinning the boy into the ground.

With renewed energy, Julia ran over, overtaking Barker as he paused to clench his knees and pant out of control.

"*Apologise*!" Jessie screamed, shaking the boy with fistfuls of his red tracksuit. "Apologise to the woman, you worm!"

"Get off me!"

"*Apologise*!"

"I said, get off me."

"I ate idiots like you on the streets for breakfast!" Jessie yelled as she shook him even harder. "Apologise, *now*!"

"*Fine*!" the boy cried, pushing Jessie's hands off him. "I'm sorry, alright?"

For a moment, Julia thought Jessie was going to plant a fist in the boy's face, but she relented and jumped off him. She scooped up Julia's bag and tossed it over the boy to her.

"Billy Matthews," Barker mumbled through his pants. "I should have known it would be *you*."

Billy's eyes widened when he saw Barker. He glanced from Jessie to Julia before darting off again. Jessie went to chase him, but Julia put her hand out and shook her head.

"I can get him!"

"Just leave it," Julia said, checking in her bag, relieved to see everything intact. "I owe you."

"Somebody had to stop him," Jessie said with a roll of her eyes. "It was like witnessing an old folks fun run watching you two."

"Maybe your gran was right," Barker mumbled as he leant against the church wall. "I'm so unfit."

"You are getting fat," Jessie said casually. "Being suspended isn't a good look for you."

Barker looked up at Jessie, his eyes narrowed and his cheeks red. Julia stared sternly at Jessie, who shrugged and shook her head as though she didn't know what she had said. Jessie might not have been blood-related to Julia, but she shared her gran's bluntness and brutal honesty. She usually appreciated it when it came to critiques of her cakes, but less so when it came to Barker's recent suspension from the police station, which seemed to be her current favourite topic to joke about. If Julia and Jessie were like mother and daughter, Barker and Jessie were more like brother and sister.

When Barker had finally caught his breath, they set off walking up the winding lane towards Julia's cottage. They reached Barker's home first, so Jessie set off on her own and left them alone.

"She didn't mean it," Julia apologised as they stood outside of Barker's gate. "You know what Jessie is like. She can be a little – *prickly*."

"It's nothing that's not true," Barker said with a small shrug as he circled his foot around on the smooth pavement. "I went to the station yesterday to see if they were any closer to deciding on my future, but nobody would speak to me. It doesn't look good, does it?"

Julia's stomach knotted inside her as she bit her lip and looked down at the ground to stare at her filthy and torn tights. It had been three weeks since Barker had been suspended and there hadn't been a day that Julia hadn't blamed herself for getting him into this mess. She was pouring her energy into baking the most perfect chocolate cake for Barker, but it didn't disguise the fact it had been her actions that had caused his suspension. Dragging him into helping her solve the murders of homeless men without official police support was a decision she was regretting every day.

"No news is good news," Julia offered pathetically.

"I've never heard of a Detective Inspector being suspended and getting their job back," he said with a small smile. "I need to face the reality of the situation."

"*Temporary* suspension," she reminded him. "That's what they said. They would be stupid to let you go."

Barker smiled at her, but she could see the worry in his eyes. He had been trying to hide it the best he could, most likely to ease her guilt, but they had been spending a lot of time together since he had been without a job, and she had seen the silence from the station chip away at his hope day by day.

There was nothing Julia could say to ease his worry, so she stood up on her tiptoes and pulled him into a hug. He nuzzled his face into her neck as she squeezed him tightly while the bright sun shone down on them. Julia wished she could make everything better, but behind her words of support, she was just as worried. She couldn't live with herself if her stupid actions lost Barker his career.

"It'll be okay," she whispered as she opened her eyes. "Everything will be -,"

Her voice trailed off when she looked ahead at Barker's cottage. She pulled away from the hug and walked around him to unhook the gate as she squinted at what appeared to be flowers on Barker's doorstep.

"What's that?" Barker asked as he followed her down the garden path.

Julia shielded her face from the sun and narrowed her eyes, her vision not what it had been in her twenties. The flowers were arranged in a circular design, with a black sash across its middle adorned with decorative silver lettering. When she figured out what the letters spelt out, all of the moisture vanished from her mouth. She parted her lips to speak, but no words came out.

"What the -," Barker mumbled.

"'*R.I.P. Barker*'," Julia read aloud in a small voice as they looked down at the flowers. "It's a funeral wreath."

CHAPTER 2

B arker paced back and forth, the wreath filling his coffee table. Julia caught herself chewing on the ends of her short nails, something she only found herself doing when she was incredibly stressed. During her divorce, she had practically chomped them down to her cuticles.

"It's probably a joke," Barker said hopefully. "Right? A joke?"

"It's not very funny," Julia said, avoiding looking at the wreath. "Who do you know that has this particular brand of humour?"

Barker paused for a moment while he stared down at the wreath, his brows tensed tightly. He shrugged and continued to pace as he ran his fingers compulsively through his hair.

"Who does this?" Barker asked, straining a laugh. "It's sick."

Julia fearfully looked down at the wreath, as if it was a bomb that might explode at any moment. It was clearly a threat. It had felt dirty and strangely weighty in her hands when she had brought it into the cottage.

The doorbell rang, offering a distraction for both of them. Julia jumped up, and Barker headed for the door, giving her a troubled look as he passed her. Alone with the wreath, she forced herself to read the words again. '*R.I.P. Barker*'. She bit hard into her index fingernail, catching the skin underneath it. Muttering under her breath, she crammed the end of her finger into her mouth, the cut stinging against the edge of her tongue.

"Julia, this is Detective Sergeant Forbes."

A man who looked to be in his late fifties walked into Barker's sitting room. He was of average height, with a large stomach pushing through his suit jacket. He had a head of thinning, grey hair, combed over from what was left on the sides. His face reminded Julia of Santa Claus, with plump red cheeks, and a grey goatee framing his smiling mouth.

"Please, call me Bradley," he said, his voice squeakier and higher pitched than Julia had expected. "I've heard a lot about you from this one. He's quite smitten."

"Thanks for coming, Bradley," Barker said, slapping the man on the shoulder. "I didn't know who else to call."

"You sounded rather rattled on the phone, old friend. Is everything okay?"

Julia stepped to the side, glancing down at the wreath as she did. Bradley squinted at the flowers before pulling a pair of thick-rimmed glasses from his upper pocket. With his eyes magnified to the size of large saucers, he leant into the wreath, teasing the sash with a finger.

"Who died?" Bradley asked. "Does that say -,"

"*Barker*," Julia said with a nod. "It was on the doorstep when we came back from the beer festival."

"Oh, how was it?" Bradley asked with a cheerful grin. "I meant to drop by, but I shouldn't really drink on the job. You know what it's like."

Bradley chuckled as he took off his glasses and slotted them back into his pocket. Julia looked desperately to Barker, wanting him to stress the seriousness of the situation.

"The thing is, Bradley, somebody left this on my doorstep," Barker continued. "Why don't I make you a cup of tea?"

"I'm parched, that would be great," Bradley said, already sitting on Barker's creaky white leather sofa. "A wreath, *eh*? Is this someone's idea of a practical joke?"

"I hope so," Julia whispered, sitting next to Bradley as Barker rushed into the kitchen.

"Not very funny, is it?"

"That's what I said."

Barker returned with a cup of tea for Bradley, a cup of coffee for himself, and a cup of peppermint and liquorice tea for Julia. She had never been more grateful for a mug of her favourite comforting beverage.

"How are things at the station?" Barker asked as he sat in his armchair, perching on the edge, dividing his attention between Bradley and the wreath.

"Oh, you know," Bradley said with a small shrug. "The usual."

Chocolate Cake and Chaos

Barker nodded and looked down into the black surface of his coffee. Julia could tell he was disappointed with Bradley's answer. He missed the station so much, he probably would have liked to hear the boring in and out details of their usual daily routines.

"Heard anything from the gaffer yet about my – *ya'know* – suspension?" Barker urged, twitching in his seat.

"You know the Chief Inspector," Bradley said with another small shrug. "Jim is a man who works at his own pace. I'm sure you'll be back soon enough, although not too quick I hope. I'm enjoying playing inspector while you're away."

"So they haven't replaced him?" Julia asked. "I'm sure that's a good sign. Right, Barker?"

Barker nodded as he sipped his coffee, his eyes firmly on the wreath. Julia could tell it didn't reassure him as much as she had hoped.

"Rough business, this suspension," Bradley said as he blew on his tea. "It will sort itself out. You watch. You don't get to be my age in the force without ruffling a few feathers."

"Have you ever been suspended?" Barker asked.

"Well, not quite. But I've had my fair share of slaps on the wrist!" Bradley replied with a soft chuckle, his bright red cheeks glowing. "Any idea who sent this thing?"

"Not that I can think of."

"Somebody you've upset?"

"You don't make many friends in our job, you know that."

"I do indeed," Bradley said, nodding in agreement as he turned and smiled at Julia. "I once had a steaming bag of – *well* – since we're in the presence of a lady, I won't go there. But it's not a job that wins you favour with the people. Anybody you arrested recently that you might have given enough reason to want to scare you?"

Barker gawked at the wreath and seemed to rack his brain for a minute.

"There's a couple," Barker said with a heavy sigh. "Peridale's a quiet place. Most of the time it is trouble with the kids from the Fern Moore Estate."

"I said they should never have built that awful place," Bradley said, his squeaky voice deepening suddenly. "Brought my house value down thousands back in the eighties. Of course, it's fine now, what with our beautiful village being so desirable, but that's not the point. Nothing good comes out of Fern Moore! They're all slippery little buggers from that place!"

"Billy Matthews, for example," Barker whispered under his breath.

"You said that name before," Julia said, her ears pricking up. "That kid who tried to steal my handbag?"

"Billy Matthews pinched your bag?" Bradley cried, shifting awkwardly in his seat, his large stomach not allowing for much movement. "Did you report it?"

"Well, he didn't steal it. We caught him, but he tried. That boy can run."

"He's a little toad," Bradley mumbled after sipping his tea. "Might as well get him a permanent cell at the station. Arrested more times than I've had hot dinners. Always let off with a caution or a fine though. I say lock him away and throw away the key, even if he is only seventeen!"

"I arrested him for stealing Denise Andrews' tractor from Peridale Farm not long before I was suspended," Barker said, suddenly snapping his fingers together. "He was here in the village today. It's got to be him!"

"I wouldn't put it past him," Bradley affirmed. "Aren't these wreath things on the pricey side? When my dad died, the flowers for his send off cost us a small fortune, and that was ten years back."

"He could have stolen another bag?" Julia offered. "He seemed to know what he was doing."

"This isn't his style," Barker said, talking himself out of it. "He's more likely to put a brick through your window. He doesn't have the brains for this."

They all sat in silence again as they tried to think of how the wreath could have turned up on Barker's doorstep. Julia didn't know the ins and outs of Barker's list of enemies, but she did know that whoever sent the wreath meant to seriously scare Barker, and if not frighten him, to warn him. She looked at the writing again, then gulped down her warm tea, not wanting to think of what it could really mean.

"It's probably nothing," Barker said, breaking the silence. "Can you look into it, old chap? *Unofficially,* of course. No point kicking up a fuss over some flowers."

"Leave it with me," Bradley said with a wink and a tap on the side of his nose. "I'll get to the bottom of this. Just call me Detective *Inspector* Forbes. Can you imagine?"

The man chuckled again, finished his tea, and stood up. He shook Julia's hand once more and headed for the door with a promise that he would look into it the second he was back at the station.

Chocolate Cake and Chaos

When he reached the front door, he stopped in his tracks and turned back to Barker, his brows pinched, a curious look in his eyes.

"I've been meaning to ask you this for a while. Does the name '*Jeffrey Taylor*' mean anything to you?" Bradley asked as he brushed down the wispy stray strands of hair on the top of his head.

Barker's face turned a deathly shade of white right before Julia. Eyes wide and jaw gritted, Barker looked more terrified by the name than he had at the wreath.

"Where did you hear that?"

"Your name came up in conversation with his earlier this week. He's just moved into the village, and they usually let us know when new releases come to our corner of the world."

"Jeffrey Taylor is *here*?" Barker asked quickly. "In Peridale?"

"Staying at Evelyn's B&B last I heard," Bradley said, the twinkle in his eye growing ever more curious. "Anything we should be worried about, boss?"

Barker appeared to be somewhere else, his eyes completely glazed as he stared through Bradley, through the door, and out of Peridale entirely. Julia nudged him, and he blinked forcefully, suddenly looking down into Bradley's face again. He forced a smile, which Julia recognised as his '*everything is fine*' smile, and shook his head.

"He's nobody," Barker said confidently. "Thanks for coming 'round. If you hear anything about my job, you have my number."

Bradley shook Julia's hand for the third time, and then left them alone in the cottage. When Barker closed the door behind him, he leant against the wood and banged his head against the frosted panel of glass.

"Who's Jeffrey Taylor?" Julia asked, her voice suddenly shaky. "Barker? Are you okay? You don't look well."

Barker's eyes glazed over again, and he seemed to be somewhere else entirely until he blinked and looked down to Julia, this time without the forced smile he had given Bradley.

"He's somebody I put away on a murder charge years ago, and last I heard he was serving a life sentence in prison," Barker said, his voice gritty. "Last time I saw him was in court for his sentencing. He said if he ever saw me again, he'd kill me, and now I guess he's in Peridale."

Julia felt a fist tighten around her heart as the village she adored suddenly became a dangerous place. She pulled Barker into the living room, sitting him back in his chair. She forced his cup of coffee into his hands. He stared down into the dark liquid, but he didn't drink it. Julia had so many questions to ask, but Barker had experienced enough stress for one day so she decided she would wait until he wanted to talk.

Instead, she went through to his kitchen and made ham and cheese sandwiches with the few ingredients in Barker's fridge. When Barker started to eat, Julia's nerves eased a little. She looked at the wreath once more, something new catching her eye. A small white tag was poking out from under the sash, which must have been disrupted by DS Forbes' brief examination. She reached out and read the stitched writing on the small tag.

"At least we know the florist," Julia said, a small smile lifting up the corners of her lips. "It's from Pretty Petals, the only florist in Peridale. I think we need to pay them a visit and get to the bottom of this ourselves."

CHAPTER 3

Mulberry Lane was the oldest known street in Peridale. Its golden Cotswold stone buildings, with sagging slate roofs, and tiny windows and doors, dated back to the 1700s. The shops and cottages contained within the winding lane were impossibly crammed together, as though they had been built on top of each other. They looked like they could crumble without a moment's notice. Despite this, they had stood the test of time.

Julia pulled up outside Pretty Petals in her aqua blue Ford Anglia. She crammed her stiff handbrake into place, and she peered through the single-paned bay window of the tiny shop. Just seeing the flowers made her feel uneasy.

"We're taking my car next time," Barker mumbled as he unbuckled his seatbelt. "This thing is ready for the scrap heap."

"She's vintage."

"She's close to death."

Julia almost laughed, but the mention of death stopped her. The wreath was still burning a hole in the pit of her stomach, as well as Barker's coffee table.

They climbed out of her petite car and stood on the narrow pavement outside the shop. They both stared at the small hand-painted sign, its peeling lettering matching that of the tiny white tag on the sash. Barker pulled it out of his pocket, and held it up to the sign, just to make sure.

"Let me do the talking," Barker said as he adjusted his stiff white collar. "It is my wreath, after all."

Julia nodded and pulled an invisible zip across

her lips, locking it at the corner. She wondered if she should have told Barker that she knew the owner of the shop, but it hadn't gone unnoticed to her that he had dressed for the occasion in a freshly ironed shirt, pressed trousers, and his shiniest shoes. She hadn't seen him dressed so smartly since his suspension, and even though he didn't have his job back yet, it warmed her to know he had a purpose again, even if it was under morbid circumstances.

A bell tinkled as Barker opened the door. He ducked into the shop, holding the door open for Julia. She stepped inside, and the scents of a dozen different brightly coloured flowers fought for her attention. A bucket of unusually bright yellow roses caught her eye, which she thought would look nice in her kitchen window. She made a mental note to pick up a bouquet for herself if things went well.

They weaved in and out of the displays towards the counter, where Harriet Barnes was peering over the top of her hot-pink glasses as she re-potted a bright orange plant with thick green leaves. Barker cleared his throat, but she held up a finger without looking at him.

"Just a second," she mumbled. "This part is *critical.*"

Julia bit her lip to stop herself from laughing.

Chocolate Cake and Chaos

With a frown deep in his brow, Barker puffed out his chest and stiffened his back, the top of his hair almost touching the low-beamed ceiling.

"*Perfect!*" Harriet exclaimed, holding the plant up to the light. "Don't you think? Nothing makes me happier than a healthy guzmania. They are beautiful, aren't they? *Oh!* Hello, Julia! What can I do for you today?"

Julia smiled her acknowledgement, but she kept true to her promise to let Barker do the talking. She stepped to the side and allowed him to take centre stage, something that caused Harriet to pull off her glasses so she could assess him suspiciously. Harriet was a regular in Julia's café, always ordering a cup of camomile tea with a slice of fruitcake. Aside from her amazing florist skills, she was well known in the village for her crazy patterned cardigans and her frizzy silver hair, which was always held up in a bun by two pencils. She was also known to call upon them if anybody ever needed something to write with.

"I was wondering if I could ask you some questions, Mrs. -,"

"*Ms.* Barnes," Harriet corrected him firmly. "I kept my husband's name after divorcing him. It was a darn sight better than Harriet Hudders. I can't tell you how many cow and milk jokes I had to endure as a child. And *you* are?"

"Detective Inspector Barker Brown," he said, a quiver in his voice. "I'm here unofficially to ask you about a wreath I think you might have made."

"I should hope it's unofficial," Harriet said casually as she put her glasses back on before flicking through a large appointment book in front of her. "I heard the new DI was fired quite recently."

"*Temporarily* suspended," Barker muttered with a cough, his cheeks blushing.

"Yes, well, even the most hopeless looking plants can be brought back from death, but root rot is still root rot, no matter what you call it. I have five minutes before I need to start on my next job. A wreath, you say?"

Barker glanced to Julia, who was still biting her tongue. He looked as though he wanted her to jump in, but she decided it was best to keep her lips locked, even if Barker had just embarrassed himself.

"Somebody left a wreath on my doorstep yesterday," Barker said as he placed the sash on the counter, the letters facing up and shining under the spotlights in the ceiling. "A funeral wreath."

"I know," Harriet said through pursed lips. "I put it there."

"Oh."

"I don't usually do deliveries for single items, but they paid extra, so I was more than happy to oblige, even if it was out of my way. I forgot you lived up that lane, Julia. I would have popped in for a cup of tea."

"The thing is, this wreath is for me," Barker said, the frustration obvious in his voice.

"Didn't you like the flowers?"

"I did, but – *well* – I'm not dead, you see."

Harriet peered over her glasses, her brow arching even higher. She looked Barker up and down, even leaning over the counter to peer at his shiny shoes.

"I can *see* that."

"Maybe there was a mix-up?" Barker asked, a glimmer of hope returning to his voice. "Is there another Barker in the village?"

"Are you suggesting I can't do my job, Mr. *Detective Inspector*?"

"No, not at all, it's just -,"

"I was given *very* specific instructions, all handwritten and *very* detailed. I followed them to the letter, including leaving the wreath on *your* doorstep yesterday morning. *Your* address was underlined and written out *very* clearly."

Barker looked to Julia again, the fear from

yesterday returning to his eyes. Julia stepped forward and decided it was time to unlock her lips to help him out.

"Can you tell us who ordered the wreath, Harriet?" Julia asked kindly.

"No can do, I'm afraid."

"Why not?" Barker asked rather loudly.

"Client confidentiality."

"They're *only* flowers!"

"And the law is *still* the law!" Harriet snapped back. "Not that you care much about the law! I'm almost *certain* it's illegal to pretend to be an officer, temporary suspension or not!"

Barker's cheeks darkened as his nostrils flared. Julia had suspected this might happen. Being a trader herself, she was familiar with the law concerning customer records and privacy, even if it was something she had never encountered in her café.

"I understand that," Julia murmured, resting her hand on Barker's arm to let him know to leave it to her. "The law *is* the law, but it's put Barker in a tricky situation. As you can understand, seeing your name on a funeral wreath can be quite distressing, and we're just trying to get to the bottom of things without wasting police time."

"You know I can't tell you, Julia."

"I know that," Julia agreed. "But the man who ordered these flowers might be -,"

"I never said it was a man," Harriet jumped in, shaking her head and pulling off her glasses.

Julia concealed her smirk, glad Harriet had fallen into her trap.

"So it was a woman?" Barker asked suspiciously.

Harriet exhaled severely, her eyes darting between them. She sighed, licked her finger, and flicked back through the book.

"Listen, I can't tell you who ordered them because quite frankly, I don't know who ordered them," Harriet said through pursed lips as she scanned her bookings. "A girl came in here on Saturday with a handwritten note and cash. She wouldn't leave a name or a contact number. I wouldn't usually stand for that, but she came in the last thing on Saturday and didn't stick around. I thought maybe her family had sent her down for a funeral that was happening on Sunday, so I put the order together and delivered it at the time that was written down."

"So she was a young girl?" Julia asked, glancing to Barker, who was looking more and more confused.

"I never said that."

"But you thought her family had sent her, which suggests she wasn't old enough to come into a florist and order funeral flowers on her own."

Harriet's lips twisted into a taut snarl, her expression growing more serious, clearly frustrated by the incessant questioning. Julia knew they didn't have long until they permanently made their way into her bad books.

"She was a teenager," Harriet said, slapping the book shut. "Thirteen, maybe younger, maybe older. It's hard to tell these days. That's all you're getting from me because that's all I know, and I'm confident that doesn't break any laws. Now if you don't mind, you've wasted enough of my time, so if you're not buying flowers, you can leave."

Julia decided against buying the yellow roses, although she made another mental note to bake a particularly rich fruitcake to give to Harriet on her next visit to the café, if she ever showed her face again. Barker led the way out of the florist, leaving Harriet to start gathering the flowers for her next job.

"Well that was a waste of time," Barker exclaimed as he shielded his eyes from the sun.

"Not necessarily," Julia said, pulling her car keys

from her bag. "We know it wasn't Jeffrey Taylor who ordered the flowers."

"I almost wished it were him. At least that would make sense."

They climbed into the car, but instead of pushing her keys into the ignition, Julia held them against the wheel and stared ahead to the end of the lane, where two men were loading a grandfather clock from the antique barn into a white truck.

"Are you going to tell me about this Jeffrey Taylor?" Julia asked, shifting in her seat to face Barker. "He seems to have you pretty rattled."

Barker glanced at her out of the corner of his eyes before running his hands down his light stubble. He looked ahead at the grandfather clock, following its journey into the truck.

"You know how Superman has Lex Luthor?" Barker asked, turning fully in his seat, his brow wrinkling deep in thought. "Jeffrey Taylor is my Lex Luthor."

"Okay?"

"He was my first case after I passed my inspector's exam eight years ago. I had just turned thirty, and I was living in Hull at the time. I had the world at my feet, and I felt unstoppable. In my first month, I was put on a serial murder case with another DI, Steven, who had thirty years experience on me. He was under pressure from the big dogs to close the case before the press grabbed hold of the story and made our jobs ten times harder. Women were turning up dead all over the city, and we couldn't figure out a pattern. It was like trying to finish a crossword puzzle without the clues. It felt like we would never get a break, and then we found Jeffrey Taylor at the scene of one of the murders. He was arrested and processed. Turns out his DNA matched one of the samples taken from another one of the victims. He didn't have alibis for any of the times of deaths, and he fit the rough profile of what we had managed to put together. Steven was sure we had our guy, so that meant I was sure. I was fresh into the job, and I didn't want to ruffle feathers by going against the grain. The evidence was purely circumstantial, and aside from the DNA, we had nothing else. It was enough though. It turned into a witch-hunt, and he got life in prison. It all happened so fast, and then when no more women were found dead, it felt like we had our guy safely behind bars."

"So what happened?" Julia asked, her stomach writhing as she edged closer to Barker, her keys clenched tightly in her fist. "Why is he suddenly out of prison?"

Chocolate Cake and Chaos

"I looked online last night and it seems new evidence recently came to light putting another man in the frame. From what I could gather, the new guy even confessed. Jeffrey's lawyers called for a mistrial, and he won. Got a healthy payout by the sounds of it too. I transferred out of Hull to London soon after the first trial, and I moved on. The case was passed on, and they never called on me, but I never forgot his words on that last day in court. '*I'll make you pay for this! I'll kill you all!*' He looked me right in the eyes when he said that. I had nightmares of him killing me for weeks, but eventually, I forgot. I had that nightmare for the first time again last night, knowing he was in Peridale. I barely slept."

"Do you think he's innocent?"

"I don't know what I think, I just know that he's here at the same time somebody warns me of my death. It's all a little too creepy to be coincidence, don't you think?"

Julia thought about it for a second, not wanting to believe that Barker could really be in danger, but also not wanting to scare him any more than he clearly already was. Instead, she reached out and grabbed his hand in hers. Their eyes connected, a smile flickering between them. A loud sound of crashing wood snapped them both back to reality, and they turned to see the grandfather clock shattering against the cobbled road.

"Coincidences do happen," Julia stated as she slotted her key into the ignition. "Maybe he's come to Peridale to start a new life like you did?"

"Or maybe he's come to ruin my new life," Barker whispered, almost under his breath.

They drove back to Barker's cottage in silence. When they pulled up outside, Julia jumped out of the car and opened her boot, pulling out a plastic cake box.

"The latest version of my chocolate cake," Julia said as she handed it over. "There's a gooey chocolate ganache centre in this one."

"You always know how to cheer me up," Barker said with a soft smile. "Join me inside for a slice?"

"I need to get back to the café," Julia said regretfully, glancing to Barker's cottage, where she knew the wreath was still sitting on his coffee table. "If I leave Jessie alone any longer she'll burn the place to the ground."

Barker kissed her goodbye, his lips lingering against hers a little longer than usual. When she climbed back in her car and drove down the lane, she peered through her rear-view mirror to see Barker standing by his gate, the cake in his hands as he watched her drive away.

For Barker's sake, Julia was going to get to the bottom of the wreath before it turned into anything else. She had no idea who had placed the order at Pretty Petals, but she did know she could find out why Jeffrey Taylor had come to Peridale.

CHAPTER 4

By the time Julia got back to the café, word of the wreath had spread around the village, no doubt thanks to their disastrous visit to Pretty Petals. When she locked the door after an unusually busy Monday afternoon, she was even more determined to get to the bottom of the strange mystery. Leaving her car parked in between her café and the post office, she sent Jessie home and set off walking across the village.

Evelyn's B&B sat on the corner of Peridale's main street, just past The Plough, and across from the small police station. It curved along the corner of the road in an L-shape, with an overgrown and wildly colourful garden at its heart, which still looked beautiful despite the dark grey sky above. Julia stood at the gate and looked up at the many windows scattered across the old cottage's frontage, knowing it was deceptively larger inside than it appeared. Despite this, a small sign poking out from a rose bush, which was in desperate need of pruning, let her know there were no rooms available.

Julia unclipped the gate and walked up to the front door holding a cardboard box containing two scones packed with cream and jam. Instead of a traditional doorbell, there was a metal chain, which Julia was instructed to pull by a small, hand-painted sign in swirling handwriting.

After Julia had pulled on the chain, which sent a melodic tune chiming throughout the cottage, the door shot open dramatically to reveal Evelyn in a loose lilac caftan with a turban secured around her head to match. A glittery diamond brooch held the turban in place, staring out into the world like a third eye.

"*Julia*!" Evelyn exclaimed. "*Come in*! Come in! Are those scones? The universe foretold that I would have an unexpected visitor. Would you mind taking off your shoes? I've only just finished shampooing the carpets this morning."

Julia obliged and kicked off her shoes. She followed Evelyn through her eccentrically decorated B&B and into the small sitting room overlooking the beautiful garden. When the B&B was closed for the long winter months, Evelyn travelled the world alone, picking up unusual trinkets and strange artefacts, which were displayed throughout her home as her own personal museum. Dot had always called the collection '*tacky*' because it wasn't the usual style in Peridale, but Julia liked Evelyn's taste in décor. It was chaotic and cluttered, but it made perfect sense for Evelyn, whose mind was similarly disordered and jumbled.

"Would you like a tarot reading, my dear?" Evelyn asked as she unclipped a small wooden box on the table. "I never had you down as a believer of tarot cards, but we're all full of surprises, aren't we?"

"No, thank you," Julia said with a polite smile as she pushed the scones onto the table. "Maybe another time. Been anywhere nice recently?"

Chocolate Cake and Chaos

"I spent the winter in Morocco," Evelyn said proudly, adjusting her turban. "I picked up a rather beautiful collection of Moroccan tea glasses there. Can I make you a cup? It will go lovely with these scones of yours!"

Before Julia responded, Evelyn scooped up the scones and floated off to the kitchen, her caftan fluttering behind her. Julia hadn't known how she was going to approach the subject of Jeffrey Taylor, but she knew a cup of tea was a good place to start.

"It's Maghrebi mint tea," Evelyn announced when she returned with a steel tray containing an oddly shaped teapot with small coloured glasses, and the scones on two plates. "I know you like your peppermint, so I'm sure you'll love this."

After pouring the tea, Evelyn scooped up one of the glasses in the palms of her hands and inhaled deeply. Her eyes flickered behind her lids, a content smile washing over her. Julia copied Evelyn's actions, surprised by the minty sweetness of the murky liquid. It calmed the nerves she had about the true nature of her visit.

"Do I detect spearmint?" Julia asked.

"Your baker's nose never fails you!" Evelyn exclaimed. "A young man who went by the name Amine introduced me to it. Amine means *faithful and trustworthy*', although I would disagree after finding out he had a wife. Alas, I was twice the boy's age, but isn't that what travel is for?"

Julia choked on her tea but attempted to pass it off as a cough. She held it in her throat, a respectful smile on her lips as her face burned bright red. Evelyn was a decade Julia's senior, but was better travelled than any other person in Peridale, and had the stories to prove it.

"It is very delicious," Julia agreed as she placed the cup back on the tray. "I'll have to see if I can buy some online."

"I brought back plenty!" she cried, waving her hand. "I'll give you a bag before you leave."

"That's very kind of you."

"Not a problem at all, my dear." Evelyn drained her cup and placed it back on the tray. "If you didn't come for a reading, and I guess you're not here for a room, not that I have any left, may I ask the purpose of your visit today? It's nice to see you, but I'm just more accustomed to seeing you in your café."

Evelyn reached out for a scone and immediately plucked it from the plate to take a large bite. With cream and jam on her lips, she chewed silently, her eyes closed once more, and an even wider grin taking over her face. Julia was happy to see her scone having the desired effect.

"I actually wanted to ask you about -,"

Before Julia could finish her sentence, the lamps flickered and turned off entirely. They sat in darkness for a moment looking up at the lights in the ceiling, but when they didn't turn back on, Evelyn sighed, ditched her scone, and forced herself up off the sofa.

"Those fuses!" she cried out. "Been on the blink ever since I got back!"

Evelyn scurried into the hall, leaving Julia alone in the sitting room. She peered out of the window as shadowy clouds rolled over Peridale, pushing the room into even further darkness. From the hallway, she heard a small bang, followed by Evelyn crying out. Julia pulled her phone out of her bag and flicked on the bright flashlight before following the B&B owner.

"Evelyn?" she called out. "Are you okay?"

"Down here," her voice echoed through an open door. "I can't see a darn thing!"

Julia pulled on the door and shone the light down into the dark cellar. Using the wall to guide her, she descended down the stone steps, every flicker of warmth leaving her body. Nerves flooded Julia's system as she realised she was surrounded by darkness in the same building as a man who had been sent to prison for murder. When she reached the bottom, she shone the light in front of her, the shadows shifting and shaping before her eyes. When the light caught Evelyn's glittery brooch, she hurried to her, glancing over her shoulder as the blackness consumed the space around her.

"I can never figure this thing out," Evelyn whispered as she flicked various switches on the fuse box. "All the labels have worn off."

Julia shone her light over the different switches, pausing on two large red ones, which were both pointing down. She forced them back up and was relieved when light flooded into the cellar from the open door at the top of the stairs.

"Happens whenever I've got a full house," Evelyn said as she adjusted her turban. "Everybody has everything plugged in at all times these days. What happened to a good book, or a conversation?"

They headed to the stairs, both of them pausing and letting out small gasps when they saw a shadowy figure standing at the top, the light illuminating only the outline. Julia shone her flashlight up to the figure, sheer fright spreading through her when she saw an almost skeletal man's face staring down at her. Tattoos crept up his arms, only stopping at his sharp jawline, darkening his presence even more.

"Jeffrey?" Evelyn cried out with a small chuckle. "You startled me!"

Julia held back and let Evelyn lead the way up the stone steps, unable to look directly at the man. She could feel his eyes trained on her, forcing the hairs on her arms to stand on end.

"Oh, *Jeffrey!*" Evelyn cried when she reached the top of the stairs. "What have I told you about taking your shoes off after you get back from your run? I've only just finished shampooing the carpets!"

Julia looked down the hall, where large muddy footprints led all the way to Jeffrey. Mud was splattered up his calves, which were saturated in tattoos, just like his arms and neck. Julia was sure every inch of his slender body was smothered in ink. She landed on his gaunt face, unsettled by his icy eyes, which felt like they were staring deep into her soul. Her stomach knotted when she noticed that the man was missing the top half of his left ear, which jutted out at an unnatural angle.

"Sorry," Jeffrey said flatly as he kicked off his shoes.

Evelyn shook her head and rolled her eyes as she leant over to pick them up. She opened the front door and placed them on the doorstep. Heavy droplets of rain beat down on Evelyn's garden from the gloomy sky above.

"I *foresaw* rain!" Evelyn cried proudly out into her garden. "The man on the TV said differently, but I could feel it coming."

She closed the door behind her, a satisfied smile on her face. Julia looked to Jeffrey to see his reaction, but she was surprised by his complete lack of expression. He suddenly reached out, and Julia flinched out of the way. When he closed the cellar door behind her, her cheeks flushed with embarrassment. She caught the letters '*I N N O*' tattooed thinly on his right knuckles, but she couldn't see the completed word on his left hand.

"There was a draft," he stated, not directing it at either of them. "I'm going up to my room."

They both watched Jeffrey climb the staircase, each step creaking under his weight as he ascended slowly. Julia didn't realise she had stopped breathing until he turned onto the landing.

"He's not a man of many words," Evelyn muttered as she tapped her chin. "But the cards see his kind soul beneath that exterior."

"Is he a guest?" Julia asked, not wanting to admit he was the reason behind her visit.

"Of sorts," Evelyn said as she floated back into

the sitting room. "He's here for three months. Of course, I gave him a discount for such a lengthy stay."

"Three months? That's a long time."

"He's looking for a home in the village, but you know what the Peridale property market is like. It's hard to find cottages up for sale here. Nobody ever leaves. You were lucky to get such a good deal with your cottage when you did."

"Do you know where he came from?"

"Hull," Evelyn said, her brows pinched together. "I think he's here to start a quiet new life. I foresee him opening up soon. A man with that many tattoos must have many stories to tell."

Julia nodded her agreement as she scooped up her handbag, somehow feeling Jeffrey's eyes staring at her through the ceiling. She thought about telling Evelyn where her new guest had come from but decided it wasn't her place to out Jeffrey's time in prison.

"Thanks for the tea. It was lovely."

"You're going already?" Evelyn asked as she settled into the sofa and poured herself another cup. "What was it you wanted to ask me?"

Julia glanced up at the ceiling as she heard movement in the room directly above them. She considered asking Evelyn more about her strange new guest, but she stopped herself, unsure of what she thought her visit would achieve.

"I just wanted to see how you were," Julia lied with a smile. "I had some scones left over, and I know how much you like them."

Luckily for Julia, Evelyn didn't seem suspicious of her kindness, which immediately made her feel guilty. Evelyn scurried off to the kitchen and returned with a small bag of green tea leaves, which she thrust into Julia's hands.

"They're best when you leave them to steep for a long time," Evelyn said with a wink. "Don't be a stranger, my dear."

Julia thanked her for the tea leaves and stepped out of the B&B, looking down at the muddy running shoes on the doorstep. She hurried down the garden path, the torrential rain soaking her through in seconds. Before she unclipped the gate, she looked back at the cottage. Through the sitting room window, she saw Evelyn settling into her sofa and inhaling a fresh cup of the Moroccan tea. Julia's eyes wandered up to the window above it, sure she had just seen movement behind the sheer curtains.

Pulling up her collar, she turned on her heels and opened the gate, feeling no closer to figuring out who had ordered the wreath. What she did now understand was why Barker was so unsettled by Peridale's newest resident. As she hurried through the rain, she still felt his icy eyes burning into her skin.

"*Julia*!" a familiar voice cried out through the darkness. "Julia! Over here!"

She squinted in the rain to see Barker huddled in the doorway of The Plough, the light above the sign casting down on his face. She hurried across the road and joined him in the shelter.

"What are you doing here?" she asked as she forced her wet hair out of her eyes.

"Went to the station, but there still wasn't any news about my job, so I thought I would come and drown my sorrows," Barker said, the stench of beer strong on his breath. "What are you doing up here?"

"I just went for a walk to clear my head," Julia lied, peering through the heavy rain to the B&B at the same time a lamp flicked on in the window above Evelyn's sitting room. "Didn't expect to get caught in a shower."

"I'm waiting for it to calm down before I walk home," Barker said, edging forward to peer up at the dark sky. "Doesn't look like it will be anytime soon."

"Well, I'm already soaked through. You could

join me on my walk home?"

Barker looked at the rain bouncing off the road, and then to Julia. He wrapped his hand around hers and pulled her out into the shower with a playful smirk. Hand in hand, they hurried through the village, defying the murky clouds circling above. Julia almost led him to her car that was parked in its usual spot next to her café, but she decided she didn't want to soak her seats through, so they set off up the winding lane. As they approached Barker's cottage, the torrential downpour suddenly slowed down, and the clouds cleared a little, allowing the last light of the evening to peek through in scattered rays.

"Typical!" Barker yelled up at the sky, his hair flat over his eyes. "Just *typical*!"

"Are you going to invite me in?" Julia asked as she wrapped her arms around her shivering body. "A cup of hot cocoa would go down perfectly right now."

"You always have the best ideas," Barker said as he unclipped his gate. "A cup of -,"

They both stopped in their tracks at the bottom of the garden path, their eyes landing on the same thing. Something else had been left on Barker's doorstep, but this time it was something far more dangerous than a wreath; it was a body.

They slowly approached the facedown figure as though not to startle him. The rain stopped completely, allowing fresh blood to pour from the back of the man's skull, dripping down his short brown hair to mix in with the moss on Barker's doorstep.

"Call the police," Barker whispered darkly, holding a hand back to stop Julia getting any closer. "And an ambulance, although I think it's too late for that."

Julia nodded and unclipped her handbag, her fingers scrambling for her phone. As she pushed the device against her ear, she stepped back and watched as Barker carefully rolled the man over. He jumped back, both hands gripping his mouth as he stared down at the wide-eyed, pale-faced man gazing loose-jawed at the clearing sky.

"It's Jim Austen," Barker mumbled through his fingers. "It's the Chief Inspector. He's my boss."

CHAPTER 5

J ulia watched the sun rise over her garden from her kitchen window as she hugged a hot cup of Evelyn's Moroccan tea. Mowgli jumped up onto the counter and stepped over the sink and gently nudged her. She tickled under his chin, and he purred rhythmically, his fluffy tail standing on end and flicking against the spider plant on the windowsill.

Chocolate Cake and Chaos

"You always know when something is wrong, don't you, boy?" Julia whispered as she set her cup down so she could pick him up. "Are you hungry?"

Mowgli clung to her robe, his claws digging through the fabric and gently pushing into her shoulder. She squeezed him tightly before setting him down by his food bowl. She glanced at the cat clock on the wall, with its swishing tail and darting eyes. It wasn't even six in the morning yet, but she emptied a pouch of cat food into his bowl all the same.

She stomped on the pedal of the bin, catching her reflection in the shiny stainless steel lid. Dark blotches circled her eyes, giving away that she hadn't been able to sleep. Every time she had tried, she had seen the glassy, lifeless eyes of Chief Inspector Austen staring up at her.

The moment she returned to her tea, a soft knock rattled the frosted pane of glass in her front door. She hurried from the kitchen and past the sitting room, where Barker was snoring soundly in the chair by the dying fire. She pulled her robe together and opened the door, relieved to see DS Forbes.

"Sorry it's so early, Julia," Bradley said, his plump red cheeks burning brightly in the early morning cold. "Is Barker still here? The forensics team has finished at his cottage."

"He's here. Please, come in."

Bradley bowed his head and stepped inside. He walked into the sitting room and cleared his throat. Barker sat up straight, his eyes springing open. He stared around the room after rubbing them, before landing on Bradley with a startled look.

"DS Forbes," Barker croaked as he ran his hands down his face. "Any news?"

Bradley sat on the couch, so Julia perched on the edge of Barker's armchair so she could rest a hand on his back. She rubbed gently, and he smiled appreciatively up at her.

"Jim's wife, Pauline, hasn't taken it too well," Bradley cooed, his voice catching. "He was due to retire next year. Their first grandchild is on the way too."

Barker dropped his face into his hands and let out a small groan. Julia gripped his shoulders to let him know that she was still there, but it didn't appear to make a difference.

"This is all my fault," Barker whispered through his fingers. "He would never have died if it wasn't for me."

"He was struck with a rock, which appeared to

have killed him quite quickly," Bradley said, reading aloud from a small notepad. "They're estimating that the time of death was between half past five and six in the evening, which means he hadn't been dead long when you found him. The rain has washed away most trace evidence, so there wasn't much forensics could pick up, but they spent all night trying anyway. Jim is – I mean - he *was* a good man. They're doing the best they can for him. So far, it's looking like a mugging gone wrong. His pockets were completely empty, and nobody has been able to find his phone. We've put a trace out for it, but if it's not used, it's not going to be easy to track down."

"This wasn't random," Barker muttered, lifting his head from his hands for the first time since Bradley had started talking. "This was about me."

"It's just a coincidence," Julia whispered, clenching his shoulder again. "There's no way you could have known."

Barker shrugged Julia off and started pacing back and forth across the hearthrug, his hands firmly clenched in his hair.

"This is connected to the wreath," Barker stated. "It's so obvious. Whoever killed Jim thought they were killing me. People always used to joke that we looked the same from behind. We got our hair cut by the same person, and we were the same height. He was coming to see me, and whoever left that wreath was waiting for me to get home, and they struck, but they got the wrong man."

"You never officially reported the wreath," Bradley reminded him. "It's better that it comes from you, rather than me. I don't want to land me in trouble too."

Bradley attempted to chuckle, but it came out flatly, leaving behind a thick silence in its wake. Barker walked over to the window and stared out at the fields ahead with his hands pressed up against the thin glass.

"This was personal," Barker said. "Somebody wanted to kill me."

"Julia's right, it could just be a coincidence," Bradley said, his tone low. "Although I have to admit, it does look suspicious. You'll both be expected to give official statements at the station later today, but you already know that."

"I suppose you want our alibis?" Barker asked coldly without turning around.

"You know it's just routine, boss."

"I was in the pub from three until six," Barker said. "Half a dozen people saw me there, including

Shelby and Bob. I was outside of the pub waiting for the rain to stop for approximately two minutes when Julia walked by. We then walked home together and – *well* – you know the rest."

"And Julia?" Bradley murmured after he finished scribbling down what Barker had just told him. "Where were you before you met up with Barker?"

Julia moved from the chair arm to the seat, shifting uncomfortably as she stared at the back of Barker's head. She didn't want to admit that she had lied to him, even if it was before they had found the poor man's body. Now wasn't the time to continue that lie.

"I was visiting Evelyn's B&B," Julia said as she stared down at her hands in her lap. "I left my café at half past five, which my lodger can account for. I then walked up to the B&B, which took around two minutes. Evelyn will be able to tell you my exact time of arrival. I wasn't sure of the time I left, but it was less than a minute before I saw Barker."

"The important thing is you're both accounted for at the time of the death, and long before it," Bradley said, snapping his pad shut after scribbling more notes. "It will make it easy to eliminate both of you really quickly so we can find the monster that did this to Jim."

Agatha Frost

Julia smiled her thanks, even if she could feel the tension radiating from Barker after learning the truth of where she had really been after finishing work.

"Can I make you a cup of tea?" Julia asked, sensing the awkward silence that was growing between them. "Or perhaps make you something to eat? You must be starving after working all night."

"I should get going," Bradley said with an apologetic smile as he pushed himself off the sofa, his large stomach hanging low over his belt. "Barker, I know people at the station would like to hear from you. They're all pretty shook up about this."

Barker nodded, but he still didn't turn around. Clutching her robe together, Julia showed Bradley to the door and thanked him for stopping by. She waited until he was at the bottom of her garden path so she could wave him off, before turning and walking slowly back into the sitting room, where the tension was almost palpable.

"Why didn't you tell me you went to check up on Jeffrey Taylor?" Barker asked as he finally turned around.

"It wasn't like that."

"What was it like then, Julia?" The sudden increase in tone took her by surprise. "Because it

68

seems like you enjoy sneaking around behind people's backs."

"I didn't know *this* was going to happen!" she snapped back, her arms folding firmly across her chest. "I just wanted to see Jeffrey for myself, and maybe ask him straight if he sent the wreath to scare you. I didn't even get a chance. He's intense, and I didn't speak two words to the man."

"I could have told you that," Barker mumbled as he brushed past her, grabbing his jacket off the back of the couch. "I told you about the Jeffrey Taylor case to *stop* you looking for information. You have *no* right sniffing around in my past, but you just can't help yourself."

Julia watched as he stormed towards the door, confused at what had just happened. She chased after him, catching the door before it slammed in the frame.

"Where are you going?" she called out as he hurried down the lane.

"To give my statement."

She stood on her doorstep, watching open-mouthed until Barker finally disappeared around the bend towards his cottage. Her closest neighbour, Emily Burns, was already in her garden, although her eyes were glued on Julia. She didn't doubt news of their argument would spread around the village before noon. When she finally turned around, she wasn't surprised to see Jessie standing in her bedroom doorway in her black pyjamas.

"Lovers' tiff?" Jessie asked sympathetically.

"To be honest with you, I don't know what that was," Julia said, shaking her head. "Sit down, and I'll make you some breakfast."

She closed the front door, and they both walked through to the kitchen arm in arm. Julia pulled eggs from the fridge, cracking them one by one into a bowl. She added salt, pepper, and a splash of milk, then poured them into a hot frying pan. As she scrambled the eggs with a fork, Jeffrey Taylor's dirty running shoes flashed into her mind, and she realised he was likely out and about in the village at the same time Jim Austen was murdered. She wished she had remembered that during Barker's outburst because it might have helped her case.

CHAPTER 6

After a nap and a shower, Julia pottered around her cottage, unable to rest because all she could think about was Barker. She hovered over his number on her phone more than once but stopped herself from pressing the green call button. He needed space and he would talk to her when he was ready.

Instead, she did the only thing she knew to do in

times of trouble; she baked. She poured her frustration and guilt into a new version of the chocolate cake, this time substituting the cow's milk for chocolate oat milk to create an even richer taste. When she finished glazing the cake in glossy icing, she dropped a glacé black cherry on top.

She took a step back from the cake to assess her work, wishing Barker were there to taste the first slice. During her baking, she had come to the conclusion that she owed Barker a big apology for going behind his back. She realised that figuring out life's jigsaw puzzles meant nothing if she didn't put those she loved before her urge to discover the truth.

With Jessie looking after the café and Mowgli chasing birds around the garden, Julia boxed up the cake and decided to turn to the one person who had always been there for her in times of need.

Cake in hand, Julia set off walking into the village. When she reached Barker's cottage, she paused to stare at the doorstep, the body still fresh in her mind. She looked into Barker's sitting room window, but he didn't appear to be home. She checked the silver watch on her wrist, wondering if he could still possibly be giving his statement.

When she reached her gran's cottage, it felt like coming home. It was a place she had found solace many times in her life. It had been there for her during her mother's death when she was a little girl, and then two decades later after her husband, Jerrad, had kicked her out of their London apartment, and it was there for her today when she needed somebody to lean on. Of course, she knew it was really her gran, and not the building that provided the deep-rooted feeling of home, but it was comforting seeing the cottage almost completely unchanged from her childhood.

Julia walked through to the sitting room and was immediately startled to see her gran on the ground, crammed between the television and the coffee table. For a moment, she thought she might have fallen, until she saw her gran's leg shoot up in the air as she lay on her side, her eyes glued to the black and white screen.

"Gran," Julia announced herself. "Are you – *okay?*"

"Get down here and join me," Dot panted. "It's a Jane Fonda. Found it in a box of tapes in the attic. Still works."

As though to prove otherwise, the videotape crackled, sending wobbly lines up and down the screen. Julia had offered to buy her gran a newer TV on more than one occasion, but Dot didn't see the point. Julia noticed the smart watch flashing her heart rate on her wrist, and she let out a small laugh at her gran's hypocrisy. She was sure if her gran somehow started a television club, she would want the biggest and latest model.

"Why is it on mute?"

"Can't stand the woman's voice," Dot exclaimed as she stood up and started to jump side to side, copying the women on the screen, who looked like they were wearing clothes of a similar neon hue to her gran's, even though they were in black and white. "You know how I feel about American accents, love. Like nails down a chalkboard. What's that?"

Dot stopped to wipe the sweat from her face with a bright green towel as she glared down at the cake. With everything else that had been going on, Julia had forgotten all about her gran's new healthy living obsession, or she had at least subconsciously hoped she would have been bored of it by now.

"It's a salad," Julia said hopefully. "It's just trapped inside a chocolate cake. You can only get to it by eating the outside first."

"I'll get *one* plate," Dot said coolly as she shuffled past Julia towards the kitchen. "I'll have a *single* bite of yours. I thought I told you not to bring contaminants into my house?"

Julia put the cake box on top of a copy of *Senior Fitness Weekly* and picked up the remote control to pause the video. Jane stopped mid jumping jack, her arms and legs floating in the air behind the crackly static.

"Where are the rest of the girls?" Julia asked when Dot returned with the single plate and two forks. "Isn't the whole point of a club to do something with other people?"

"They're too weak," Dot said bitterly, her wrinkled lips pursing tightly. "They can't keep up with me!"

"Don't you think you might be being a bit hard on them? Not everybody has your – how shall I put this – *zest* for life?"

"Somebody has to be hard on those old biddies, or else we all rot and die! You need to stay sharp and active, especially at my age, Julia. You should watch that documentary I told you about. It will make you see things *very* differently."

Julia was sure it would, but getting fit and losing weight were the last things on her mind. She pulled the cake out of the box and instead of cutting a slice, she dropped it onto the plate and started digging from the middle.

"I suppose you heard of the murder outside of Barker's cottage?" Julia asked through a mouthful of the milky cake.

"Emily Burns called first thing this morning when she saw all of the police. I went to the café the second it opened and Jessie – *well*, she told me what happened between you and Barker, so I thought you might like some time alone. I knew you'd come when you were ready."

"That's what I'm hoping happens with Barker," Julia said, glancing at the clock as it ticked past three in the afternoon. "He said I couldn't help sticking my nose into things."

"He's *not* wrong," Dot murmured as she dug her fork into the middle of the cake. "The difference is, you're not an idle gossip. You only stick your nose into the worthy causes. I don't doubt that whatever you did was because you thought it was the right thing to do."

"I did, at the time."

"Then that's all that matters."

"How do you know if somebody is keeping something from you?" Julia asked as she stared down at the cake on the end of her fork. "I don't think I know Barker as well as I want to believe that I do."

"Why do you say that?"

"The way he reacted this morning, it felt like something more. He told me not to go digging in his past, but I only went looking for something based on what he had said to me."

"What did you do?"

Before Julia could answer, she was interrupted by the roaring sound of a lawn mower engine starting up. She looked out of the window to the village green, expecting to see somebody trimming the neat grass, but there was nobody there.

"I've got a gardener in the back," Dot explained. "I've let it get out of hand. So, what did you do?"

Julia tried to think of what she had done, but the spluttering of the lawn mower working through the long grass was too distracting. She crammed the chocolate cake into her mouth, her brows furrowing tightly.

"I thought you fired your garden guy for accidentally cutting the heads off your tulips?"

"I got someone new," Dot said, waving a hand dismissively. "Evelyn recommended him. Does it matter?"

"No," Julia said with a shake of her head. "I thought you didn't like Evelyn? I thought she was too '*wacky*' for you?"

"Oh, she is. When she caught me looking at the

ads in the post office window, she said she *foresaw* that I needed help. What a load of old *codswallop*! If that woman has the sight, then she needs her eyes tested. The man she recommended was charging a fair price, and quite frankly, I'm on a budget after buying this gizmo on my wrist."

Julia crammed another forkful of cake into her mouth, unable to shake the uneasy feeling in her stomach. Instead of ruminating, or asking her gran more questions, she ditched the fork and the cake, and walked through to the dining room, where she saw Jeffrey Taylor forcing a lawn mower through the overgrown grass.

"Julia? What has gotten into you?" Dot cried as she chased after her. "It's all that sugar and fat in the cake! It's pushing you over the edge!"

"I'm all right, Gran," Julia insisted, shaking her gran's hands off her. "Your new gardener is the reason Barker is mad at me."

"Julia, please tell me you didn't -,"

"*Gran!*" Julia cried, cutting her off before she could finish her sentence. "Barker knows Jeffrey. He sent him to prison."

"Jeffrey sent Barker to prison?"

"Barker sent *Jeffrey* to prison," Julia said with a sigh. "He was sentenced to life on a serial murder charge."

"There's a murderer in my garden?" Dot muttered, her hand clasping over her mouth. "Call the *police*! Call the *army*! Call *somebody*! He's in possession of a dangerous weapon right this second! Do you know how fast those blades travel? Fast enough to chop off my poor head!"

"Calm down, Gran," Julia said, grabbing her by the shoulders to give her a good shake. "He was released because they found that he had been wrongly convicted."

"So he's innocent?"

"Maybe."

"*Maybe* isn't good enough, my dear!"

"In the eyes of the courts, he is," Julia said, narrowing her eyes on Jeffrey as he rammed the lawn mower over a tough patch of grass. "I'm not so sure. He makes me feel uneasy."

"Why is he in Peridale, anyway?"

"Starting a new life, apparently," Julia whispered as her gran joined her to stare out of the window. "That's what Evelyn said."

"Evelyn talks a lot of *tosh*! She probably foresaw it and skipped asking him," Dot snapped with a roll of her eyes. "Oh, it's quite exciting though, isn't it? A convicted serial killer here in Peridale? Certainly beats any other gossip I've heard this week. Well, aside from the murder, of course. Do you think he was the one who bashed Jim's head in with the rock?"

"*Gran!*"

"*What?*" Dot cried, waving her hands in the air. "You young 'uns are too sensitive. Can't call a spade a spade these days without you getting on your FaceTweet and SnapBook, or whatever they're called. Not everything needs a petition you know, sweetheart! I'm going to make him a cup of tea. He might have some juicy prison stories."

Dot hurried off to the kitchen, leaving Julia to watch him work. He pushed the mower towards the end of the garden, the spluttering noise growing further away. When he reached the bottom of the long stretch of grass, he pulled his grey, sweat-stained T-shirt over his head to wipe down his face. In the jumble of dark tattoos covering the length and breadth of his body, a skull and crossbones between his shoulder blades jumped out at her, sending a shiver down her spine. She stared into the shadowy, soulless eyes of the inked drawing, unable to look away. Through the heat lines of the afternoon, she was sure she saw its mouth smirking at her.

Chocolate Cake and Chaos

Jeffrey suddenly looked over his shoulder, his icy blue eyes piercing across the garden and staring deep into Julia's, as though he had known she had been standing there watching him the entire time. She took a step back into the darkness of the dining room, turning her attention to the kitchen while her gran poured milk into a cup of tea.

"I'll take that out," Julia said, putting her hands on the cup.

"You will *not*!"

Julia firmly pulled the cup from out of her gran's hands and hurried out of the open back door, closing it behind her. She glanced through the kitchen window, where her gran was glaring at her with her mouth ajar. Julia had more important things to extract from the mysterious newcomer than prison stories.

"I've brought you a cup of tea," Julia said, applying her friendliest smile. "Thought you might be thirsty."

Jeffrey took the cup from her, ignoring the handle and grabbing it around the middle as though it wasn't hot. Without blowing, he took a deep gulp of the tea, finishing half of it in one go. He tossed the other half into the grass before passing the cup back to Julia. She stared down at the dregs of sugar at the bottom of the cup, unsure of what to say.

"We met yesterday," Julia offered, smiling even wider. "Remember? At Evelyn's?"

"I remember," he replied flatly.

"I didn't realise you were a gardener."

"I'm not."

"Oh," Julia mumbled, her smile wavering. "Well, you're doing a great job. I hope my gran is paying you well. You have to be pretty fit to push a mower through this grass. I'm sure it grows twice as thick as the rest of the grass in Peridale, but I'm sure you're more than fit enough, what with your running."

Jeffrey's expression didn't waver, his piercing eyes not looking away from hers. She was sure she hadn't seen him blink yet. She waited for him to speak, but nothing left his lips.

"My gran is suddenly into fitness. I'm thinking of joining her for a jog, but I never know where to go. Where do you go running?"

Julia almost wanted to take the words back. It was painfully obvious that her embarrassing attempt to extract information from the man wasn't going to work. When she finally noticed him blink, she eased a little.

"Around," he said. "I should get on with this."

Chocolate Cake and Chaos

"Of course," Julia said with a nod, almost glad of a reason to step back. "Good luck with the rest of it."

She turned around and hurried back to the cottage, her face scrunched up in humiliation. She almost wished she had just let her gran take out the tea to badger him about his time in prison. Before both of her encounters with Jeffrey, she had gone in with a clear idea of what she had wanted to find out, but he was so peculiar, it scrambled her brain and turned her into a nervous wreck.

"I know who you are," he called across the garden, stopping her dead in her tracks.

"I'm sorry?" she replied, turning around.

"I know who you are," he repeated as he rubbed his T-shirt across his tattooed chest. "You're Brown's girlfriend."

Julia's heart stopped, and her cheeks burned brighter than they ever had before. She opened her mouth to defend herself, but no words rolled off her tongue. She felt like she stood there for hours, staring wide-eyed across the garden at the tattooed stranger, unable to form a single sentence in her mind. It wasn't until he turned and continued mowing the grass that she summoned the strength to run back into her gran's cottage.

"Well?" Dot demanded. "What did he say?"

"Nothing."

"*Nothing?*" Dot cried. "You're useless, my dear! Nobody knows about our new criminal resident yet, and I want first dibs on the gossip. Give me that cup. I'm trying again!"

Julia handed over the cup and walked through to the sitting room to grab the rest of her chocolate cake. She looked down at it, but it just reminded her too much of Barker, so she left it behind. She knew it would probably find its way into her gran's bin, but she had no other use for it right now.

Leaving her gran to badger the gardener, she stepped out into the daylight. She looked across the village green, considering helping Jessie close the café for the day, but the thought of having to face the people who had heard she was the one who had found Jim's body put her off. Instead, she headed off to the station to give her statement, knowing the sooner she could put the whole event behind her, the better.

CHAPTER 7

After a long and chaotic shift at the café, Julia was more than pleased to see Barker sitting on her garden wall when she pulled up outside her cottage. She could barely contain her smile as she climbed out of the car.

"I'll leave you two to it," Jessie mumbled, pulling her house keys from her pocket. "Try not to bite each other's heads off again."

Barker chuckled softly and dropped his head. When he looked up and met Julia's eyes, she knew everything was going to be okay between them. She looked down at the plaster on her hand where she had almost sliced off a finger cutting a slice of toast because she hadn't been able to concentrate all day.

"I was just sitting in The Plough staring into a pint, wondering why I wasn't here with you," he whispered, reaching out and grabbing Julia's hand. "I owe you an apology."

"So do I."

"You were just trying to help," he said with a quick wink. "I should never have talked to you like I did. To say the last couple of days have been stressful is an understatement."

"Do you want to come inside? There's a slice of chocolate cake with your name on it."

"I was wondering if you wanted to come with me to the Fern Moore Estate?" Barker asked as he pushed away from the wall. "DS Forbes kindly informed me that Billy Matthews was caught trying to sell a phone he claimed to have found in a bush. I'll give you one guess to figure out whose phone it was."

"Jim's?"

"*Bingo.*"

Chocolate Cake and Chaos

"They arrested him? Is it safe to talk to him now?" Julia asked cautiously. "I don't want you to get in any more trouble."

"At this rate, I'll be lucky to get my job back now. Jim was the only person who was really in my corner. I owe it to him to at least try and piece this together."

Julia didn't need to hear any more. In minutes, they were driving out of the village and towards Fern Moore. She turned to Barker and couldn't help but smile. They might have only been giving each other the silent treatment for one day, but it only confirmed the love she felt for him even more. There was nowhere she would rather be than by his side.

Fern Moore Estate was just outside of Peridale, but very separate. If you asked any villagers if Fern Moore was part of Peridale, they would deny it until they were blue in the face. The estate had always had a troublesome reputation. As a teenager, Julia and her school friends were advised to stay away if they didn't want to get into any fights. As an adult, she drove past it on the A roads, happy to look in the other direction. Their search for Billy Matthews was her first official visit to the area.

The estate consisted of two large U-shaped

buildings looking over two courtyards, which had been built in the early 1980s and housed hundreds of families in small flats. External walkways ran along the fronts of the flats, acting as makeshift balconies. The courtyards appeared to be a meeting place for the residents, not unlike Peridale's village green. Instead of regularly trimmed pristine grass, Fern Moore's common area housed an out-of-date, vandalised, and graffiti-covered children's play-park, which didn't look safe for any child to be playing on. Julia wasn't surprised to see the gate padlocked, and the park empty and full of beer cans.

"Billy Matthews is up there," Barker whispered, pointing to a flat at the end of one of the walkways on the second floor. "Let's not stick around too long."

Julia nodded and hurried to keep up with Barker as they walked towards a narrow stairway, passing a lift that looked like it hadn't been in use for years. Just like the park, graffiti covered so much of the stairwell that it was almost impossible to recognise the original wall colour underneath.

Their heels clicked on the concrete walkway as they passed all of the flats, each of them with a single-paned window and a blue front door, which didn't look much thicker than plywood. Julia heard snippets of conversations, arguments, and television programmes as they rushed towards the last flat, neither of them wanting to linger for too long. Some of the flats looked more well kept than others, with clean curtains in the windows, and flower baskets decorating the frontage, but most looked as rundown as the dated complex felt. Julia loved her wide-open countryside too much to imagine ever living in such a confined space.

"I'm here so often they should cut me a key," Barker mumbled as he rapped his knuckles loudly on the door. "Billy Matthews wouldn't know how to stay out of trouble if his life depended on it."

A woman screeched behind the door, her voice seeming to bounce and echo into every corner of the estate. The door cracked open, a chain stopping it from opening more than a couple of inches. A cloud of cigarette smoke greeted them, and Julia tried her best not to cough. When it cleared, they saw the squinting face of a woman in her late-thirties, clutching a cigarette between her lips, smoking it hands-free while she balanced a white-haired toddler on her hip. The woman was wearing a stained nightgown, which Julia guessed she had been wearing since that morning, rather than having just changed into it.

"What?" she barked through a hoarse cough. "What do you want?"

"We're looking for Billy, Sandra," Barker said, stepping forward as he glanced awkwardly to Julia. "I'm Barker Brown. We've met several times."

"Whatever he's done, he's not here," she cried over the sound of the TV, rolling her eyes heavily before looking over her shoulder. "*Turn that racket down!*"

Julia peered into the messy living room, spotting a young teenage girl with bright red hair sitting on the couch, a remote control clasped in her hands. Instead of turning the TV volume down, she cranked it up.

"Do you have any idea where Billy is?" Julia asked over the noise, applying her friendliest smile.

"Even if I knew, love, I wouldn't tell you," Sandra said with a smirk. "We don't snitch on our own 'round here, especially not to the police."

"We're not here on official business," Barker said, not seeming to want to admit he was no longer an active DI. "We just wanted to ask him some questions about his arrest earlier today."

"What arrest?" Sandra snapped as she puffed smoke expertly out of her nose like a dragon.

"Do you have any idea what time Billy will be

back?" Barker asked, avoiding her question.

"If you're not police, clear off."

With that, Sandra slammed the door shut and disappeared back into her flat. The TV suddenly turned off, followed by loud shouting, and then a girl crying. They lingered for a moment, but it was evident they weren't going to find the information they had wanted from Billy's mother.

"She's not the most – *cooperative* mother," Barker said tactfully.

"You could say that."

They shared a smile before heading back towards the stairwell. Julia felt like they were on a wild goose chase, following breadcrumbs into the dark. She knew there was every chance Jim's death was the mugging gone wrong that DS Forbes suspected, but she also knew it was likely to be something more personal. If somebody had thought they were murdering Barker, she knew it would only be a matter of time before that person tried to finish what they had started.

"What now?" Julia asked as they reached the bottom of the stairs.

"I don't know," Barker said as they emerged from the stairwell. "*Hey*! Get away from that car!"

Barker darted towards a gang of boys who had

gathered around Julia's Ford Anglia. Her heart stopped when she noticed one of them trying the door handles. Startled by Barker, most of them scattered, apart from three, who stepped back with dangerous smirks on their faces. The boy who appeared to be the leader of the group was wearing a black cap, a blue matching tracksuit with three white stripes running down either side, and bright white trainers. Under the shadow of the hat, Julia recognised the boy's face.

"I should have known it would be you," Billy snorted as he slurped beer out of a can from the side of his mouth. "PC Plod and his sidekick, coming to save the day."

Julia found herself clutching her handbag closer to her body as she approached the gang. Billy caught her eyes and smirked, his brows darting up and down. With the clothes and the can of beer, it was easy to forget he was still a child.

"Just the boy I was looking for," Barker said smugly, stuffing his hands into his trouser pockets. "Would you mind stepping away from the lady's car, Billy?"

"It's crap anyway." Billy swigged from his beer can and spat the beer across Julia's windshield. "I've seen tins of beans more advanced than this hunk of junk."

Julia bit her tongue, knowing it wasn't the right time to jump in and defend her beloved vintage vehicle. She looked to Barker, who stepped forward to stand between the boys and the car.

"Heard you were arrested yesterday, Billy," Barker said firmly, his arms folded protectively across his chest. "Trying to sell a dead man's phone? That's low, even for you."

"I was framed, wasn't I, lads?"

Both of his friends grumbled their agreement, their arms and chests puffed out, despite all being on the thin side. They stayed two steps behind Billy, apparently knowing their place behind their leader.

"That's always the story with you, Billy," Barker said with a small laugh. "You never just own up to anything, do you?"

"That's because pigs like you always blame me for everything," Billy said, glugging the last of the beer before crunching the can in his hand and tossing it into the ruined park. "You lot like to pin things on lads like us."

"And what are '*lads like you*'?" Barker asked.

"Street lads. You think because we dress like this we're criminals."

"But you *are* criminals," Barker said flatly. "You

alone have a criminal record longer than my arm, and that's not even including your scrawny henchmen."

The two boys took a step forward, their arms puffing out even more as they glared under their caps at Barker. Julia found their appearance more amusing than menacing, even if she wouldn't want to cross them in a dark alley.

"Is this your bird?" Billy scoffed, stepping forward and walking around Julia. "Bit fat, isn't she?"

"*She* has a name," Julia snapped as she straightened out her pale blue dress. "Would you speak to your mother like that?"

"Probably," Billy said, which caused a snicker among his friends. "I found the phone, alright? I didn't know whose it was. Some pig caught me trying to flog it down the Marley Street Market. I wasn't to know it was a dead man's."

"I heard you found the phone in a bush," Barker said firmly, cocking his head back to stare down at the boy. "Sure you didn't take it from his body after you hit him over the head with a rock?"

"Why would I want to do that?" Billy snorted. "Didn't even know the poor bugger."

"Because you thought he was me."

"Don't flatter yourself, PC Plod."

"That's DI Brown, to you."

"Not from what I heard," Billy said, walking behind his two friends and slapping them both on the shoulders. "The streets have been talking about you getting sacked. Best news we've heard all year!"

Barker gritted his jaw, his cheeks burning bright red, just as they had when Harriet had called him out on his suspension. Julia stepped forward and rested her arm on his shoulder, but he shook it off to start circling the boys.

"The thing is, Billy, you *are* a criminal," Barker said coldly, making sure to look in the kid's eyes at all times. "It's only a matter of time before you do something that's going to land you behind bars for good, and when that day comes, the streets will be a safer place."

"Yeah, well, until then, I'll just keep doing what I do with my lads."

The two boys mumbled their agreement as they watched Barker circle them once more.

"It's no life, is it, Billy?"

"So what? Nothing else to do."

"Where did you get the phone?"

"I told you, I found it."

"But where?"

"In a bush at the bus station," Billy said, holding back his laughter. "What does it even matter? They let me go. They have CCTV footage of me finding the phone. I didn't kill that pig, even if it is one less of you on the streets."

Barker suddenly stopped in his tracks, the whites of his eyes shining brightly. Julia was sure he was about to lay his hands on the kid, so she jumped in between them and rested her hands on Barker's face. He looked through her for a moment, before finally meeting her eyes. She shook her head and pulled him towards the car.

"Wish it would have been you that had taken a brick to the head," Billy said before spitting at Barker's feet. "After what you did, it's the least you deserve. C'mon, lads. These two losers aren't worth our time. I heard there's a party at Trisha's flat."

With that, the trio headed towards the nearest stairwell and disappeared, not before turning and smirking at Barker one last time. Julia rested her hand on his chest, letting him know they weren't worth it.

"I'm all right," Barker said after shaking his head. "He's usually even worse than that."

Julia pulled him over to a green steel bench outside of the closed park. The paint had worn away where people had scratched their names in more than one place to reveal the rusting metal underneath. They both perched on the edge of the bench, looking up at the sky as pale pink leaked into the horizon.

"What did Billy mean when he said '*after what you did*'?" Julia asked, resting a hand on his.

"How long have you got?" Barker whispered with a small laugh. "I've arrested that kid a dozen times since moving to Peridale. I think the boys at the station had given up on him, but I wasn't going to let things slide."

"Do you think he murdered Jim?"

"I don't know," Barker said with a sigh as he stared up at the fading sky. "I can't believe this is happening. When I first came to this village, a lot of people at the station weren't happy about me coming in from the city. They thought they should have promoted from within the station, but Jim championed me. He was behind me the whole way, even when he had to suspend me. He was probably just coming to see how I was doing that night. That's the type of guy he was. He would give you the clothes off his back if you asked him. He didn't deserve to go out like that. That should have been me."

Julia bowed her head. She felt selfish for being glad that it wasn't Barker who had died, but she didn't want to tell him that. She couldn't imagine how she would have reacted if it had been Barker that she had found blood soaked on the doorstep that night.

"When I went to Evelyn's B&B to talk to Jeffrey, he wasn't there," Julia said.

"You don't have to explain."

"Just listen," Julia interrupted him. "He wasn't there at first, but he came back around six, just before it started raining. His shoes were all muddy. Evelyn said he had been out for a run, and even though he didn't correct her, he didn't say anything to the contrary."

"You think he was in the village at the time of the murder?"

"I'm almost sure of it," Julia said, edging closer to him. "He was at my gran's yesterday doing her gardening, and I tried to talk to him to establish an alibi, but he didn't give me anything. He did, however, know that you and I were connected. He called me '*Brown's girlfriend*'."

"He always called me '*Brown*'," Barker muttered. "Just talking about Jeffrey is bringing back so many bad memories. I thought he was firmly in my past with the rest of it, but here he is, swanning around the village like he owns the place."

"The rest of it?" Julia asked.

Barker looked at her before looking up to the sky again as dusk set in. He stood up and held his hand out for her.

"A story for another day," he said. "Have you told anyone about Jeffrey's ill-timed run?"

"I told the police everything in my statement yesterday."

"Good," Barker said with a firm nod. "We have to trust they know what they're doing because right now, all I want to do is go back to the village, grab a bottle of wine from the shop, and curl up on the couch with you and a DVD."

Julia rested her head on his shoulder as they walked back to the car under the setting sun. Barker's proposition sounded like the best thing she had heard all week, and for one night, she was going to forget all about the wreath, Jim's murder, and Jeffrey Taylor.

"Can I pick the DVD?" Julia asked as she unlocked the car.

"Yes, but I'm not watching *Breakfast at Tiffany's* again."

"But it's my favourite film."

"And *Die Hard* is mine," Barker said as he climbed into the car. "But we haven't watched that three times, have we?"

"As long as I'm with you, Barker, I'll watch *Die Hard* one hundred times."

"I'm going to hold you to that," Barker said with a wink as he pulled his seatbelt across his chest. "Did you mention something about chocolate cake earlier? I'm starving."

CHAPTER 8

It was a rare occasion that Julia took a lunch break and an even rarer one that she left the café and went somewhere else to eat. Her lunch usually consisted of a hurriedly made sandwich, which she would eat in small bites in the kitchen in between serving customers, but she had been given a lunch invite that she couldn't refuse.

Still in her apron and covered in flour, she ran

across the street to The Plough where Barker was already perched on a bench waiting for her. She glanced back to the café, hoping Jessie would be okay on her own despite the sudden lunchtime rush.

"I can't stay long," Julia said, glancing at the door. "Is he here?"

"You've got flour in your hair," Barker said as he reached out to brush it away. "He's already inside."

They walked into the old pub, the musky smell of old wood and beer hitting Julia. To her surprise, it was already quite busy, but she didn't recognise many of the faces, so she guessed they were tourists passing through for the day, unlike her café, which was filled with regular faces today. The one face she did recognise was that of DS Forbes, who was already tucking into a meat and potato pie, which he had drowned in gravy.

"Sit down!" Bradley exclaimed, standing up a little, his large stomach hitting the table. "I hope you don't mind, but I already ordered. I was starving! They've got me working double time since – *well*, you know."

Bradley scooped up a large forkful of the pie filling and crammed it into his mouth. A blob of gravy trickled down his chin, landing on the paper napkin he had tucked in his collar to protect his white shirt. Julia found the man comical, but she wasn't confident of his inspector skills. She had been more than a little intrigued when he had called Barker and asked them out to lunch to inform them of the latest developments.

"I'll have whatever Bradley has," Barker said to Shelby when she came over to take their orders. "And a pint of whatever craft beer you have at the moment."

"I'll have the same, but make my drink orange juice," Julia said without looking at the menu. "I need to go back to work with a clear head."

"I need a pint to take the edge off," Bradley said after sipping his beer, which he also spilt down his front. "The stress of this case is making me lose my hair!"

Julia looked up to his balding head, which shone brightly under the light, wondering if it was possible to notice if the little hair he had left at the sides was thinning.

"Have you heard about Jim's funeral?" Bradley asked. "Happening on Sunday. They released his body last night."

"So soon?" Barker muttered, glancing awkwardly to Julia.

"They didn't have much to discover in the postmortem, did they?" Bradley said with a small shrug, his voice catching a little. "Pauline wants us all there in our uniforms for his send-off. It's what Jim would have wanted."

"These developments?" Barker asked, eager to shift the course of the conversation. "Must be pretty good if you wanted to meet us here."

"It is need-to-know information," he mumbled through a mouthful of the pie as he tapped the side of his nose. "But I trust you both understand what I'm telling you doesn't leave this pub."

"Of course," Barker said.

"Absolutely," Julia added.

"Good." Bradley took another deep gulp of his pint, followed by another mouthful of pie, before speaking again. "Billy Matthews' alibi has fallen apart. He said he was with his two cronies, but we've arrested them for nicking a car without him on the night of the murder. Shilpa from the post office came forward with her CCTV recordings this morning when she heard about the murder. Her security camera reaches out to the bottom of the lane leading up to your cottage. Caught Billy Matthews heading up that way at about half past five, putting him there at Jim's death."

"Have you arrested him?" Barker asked, edging

Chocolate Cake and Chaos

forward.

Shelby returned with the plates of food, followed by the drinks. Barker followed Bradley's lead and drowned his pie in gravy, but Julia much preferred to taste her food, so she decided to go without. She pricked the thick crust to let a little of the steam escape as Bradley took the pause in conversation to wolf down more of his pie.

"It's all circumstantial so far," Bradley said. "You know how it is, boss. Billy was caught trying to flog Jim's phone down at the market, but CCTV proved his story about finding it in a bush at the bus station. Then he's caught near the crime scene around the time of the murder, but he wasn't the only one. We don't have anything we can pin to him quite yet."

"Did you look into Jeffrey Taylor?" Barker asked, his voice lowering to a whisper.

"Ah," Bradley said, finally finishing his pie and wiping his mouth with the napkin tucked in his shirt. "Your old friend. He's a fascinating character with a real motive, but it's difficult to pin this on him too. I checked into what you said about Jeffrey being out and about in the village during the rain, and it seemed he ran past every CCTV camera that we've checked in the village. He did run up your lane at around quarter to, but he was not seen again until he passed the station camera around six and headed into the B&B. He must have run up by Peridale Farm and circled the long way. I checked in with Peridale Farm, but they're living in the dark ages and don't have any cameras. Here, I have a video on my phone."

Bradley wiped his gravy-covered fingers on his trousers before pulling his phone from his pocket. He flicked through his files before turning the screen around and pressing the play button. A grainy video started to play, and it took Julia a second to recognise it as the perspective of the village from the post office. It pointed out at the village green, her gran's cottage, and the small lane leading up to their cottages. First, a man in a red tracksuit and black cap, who was unmistakably Billy Matthews, walked up the road while looking down at his phone. He disappeared from view, and then the footage jumped to Jeffrey Taylor jogging across the village green and towards the lane as he checked his watch. Neither man looked like they were on their way to commit murder, but Julia knew it was possible they hadn't headed in that direction with the intention of killing Jim, rather taking the opportunity when they thought they saw Barker alone on his doorstep.

"And the wreath?" Julia asked, not wanting to

let them forget about it. "Did you find out who ordered that?"

"I found out about your little visit, but of course, that was before you officially reported it, and before – *ya'know* – Jim's death. I got a description of the girl who placed the order, but aside from that, we haven't been able to identify her yet."

"Are you still suspecting that it's connected?"

"Honestly? No," Bradley said as he pushed his plate away and rested a hand on his stomach. "We're looking into the angle of a random attack. We found Jim's wallet in the bush where Billy found the phone, and they had taken his cash and cards."

"Why ditch the phone?" Julia asked.

"Phones are traceable," Barker said. "Usually when there is a mugging, the victim can walk away to tell the tale, so tracing the phone isn't necessary. When it turns into a murder case, it's one of the first things the police do, so the murderer is likely to dump the phone the first chance they get."

"Did you check the bus station CCTV?" Julia asked.

"We did," Bradley said with a nod as he dabbed at his hot, bright red cheeks. "It was dark and raining on and off that night. We're looking into a couple of suspicious people who were around that area at that time, but again, it's proving difficult to pin down. This isn't the first attack of its kind recently though. There have been a spate of muggings and break-ins across the Cotswolds in the last couple of weeks, so we're looking into those cases to see if we find anything in common."

"You won't find anything," Julia said firmly, not realising she had spoken the words at the same time she had thought them. "This wasn't random. Murder doesn't happen on your doorstep for the sake of a mobile phone and a wallet. Surely if they wanted something of value they would have broken into the cottage after killing Jim? Was anything taken, Barker?"

"Not that I know of."

"This wasn't random," Julia confirmed. "Somebody wanted to kill Barker, and they hit the wrong man, which means Barker's life is still at risk."

"Has anybody threatened your life since, boss?" Bradley asked, turning to Barker.

"No," Barker said uneasily. "Not yet."

"Then there's no reason to suspect they will, right?" Bradley replied, nodding resolutely. "We're looking into many interesting lines of inquiry, so I'm sure we'll crack the case in no time!"

It took everything in Julia's power not to sigh

with exasperation. Bradley seemed like a lovely man, and she was sure in any other circumstance she would enjoy his company, but in the capacity of acting Detective Inspector, she found him infuriating. He felt more like a comedy character plucked from a detective show, than a man capable of solving a real murder case.

When the conversation turned to football and beer, Julia knew Bradley had told them everything he knew. She had expected to hear some grand revelation, but she was left hungry for more information, and also full from too much meat and potato pie. She wasn't surprised Billy's alibi had fallen through, nor was she surprised Jeffrey was in the area, but Bradley was right about the evidence so far being purely circumstantial. Until she discovered a real clue, it was going to be difficult to prove if either man was truly involved in the murder.

She finished her orange juice and excused herself. She thanked Bradley for the invite, and he stood up, knocking the table with his stomach once more. Barker walked her to the front door, his hand on the small of her back.

"He's better at his job than he comes across," Barker whispered to her, having sensed her apparent reservations of his abilities. "You just need to get to know him. He's one of the better ones we have. It just takes him a little longer to funnel his energy. He'll get there."

"I'm sure he will," Julia said, forcing a smile. "Go and finish your pint. I need to get back to work anyway."

"I'm going to ask if he's heard anything about my job," Barker said after kissing her on the cheek. "I feel like I should have heard something after Jim."

"I'm sure it will be any day now," she said as encouragingly as she could. "Will I see you at my cottage tonight?"

"Only if I'm invited."

"You're always invited," Julia leant in and kissed him on the lips. "See you later."

Barker winked at her and walked back to the table. Julia stepped out into the daylight, shielding her eyes from the bright sun. She dusted a little flour off her apron as she walked past a group of tourists drinking beer at one of the outside tables. She smiled at them before heading to the edge of the road. Traffic in Peridale was usually quiet, but she looked both ways as she always did. When she looked in the direction of the B&B, she saw a familiar shade of red moving amongst the tall flowers in Evelyn's garden. If it hadn't been for the CCTV footage she had just seen, she might not have thought anything of it, but she had Billy Matthews fresh on her mind.

Julia crossed the road so that she was opposite the B&B, not wanting to arouse suspicion. She walked past the police station, smiling to a young constable she recognised from around the village. When the constable jumped into a police car and pulled out of the small station car park, she took her opportunity to cross the road without being seen.

Ducking under the B&B wall, she peered over the '*NO VACANCIES SIGN*' to see Billy creeping around the side of the cottage, glancing over his shoulder as he did. Julia followed him around the building, staying as low to the ground as she could, but sure that her curls were darting up and down; she just hoped the flowers were enough to hide them.

Luckily for Julia, the cottage was on the street corner so she could see directly into its entire garden. She saw Billy knock on the backdoor as he skittishly made sure nobody was watching him. He looked in Julia's direction, forcing her to duck out of view. She heard the door open, but she didn't dare look.

As it turned out, she didn't need to see the person on the other side of the door to know who it was. In the peace and quiet of the sleepy village afternoon, she heard a very clear voice say something very familiar.

"I foresaw you would come, Billy," she heard Evelyn say. "Come in. Did anybody see you?"

The door closed, stopping Julia from hearing the rest of the conversation, not that she needed to. She tried to think of an innocent reason Billy would be visiting Evelyn, but he didn't seem like the type of person who would enjoy a cup of Moroccan tea and a tarot reading. Julia didn't want to think Evelyn was capable of anything other than friendly conversation, but her mind was taking her to dark places.

Before she could dwell on them any longer, somebody tapped on her shoulder, causing her to jump up. She was relieved to see it was just her gran, who was wearing her brightest neon workout clothes yet.

"Dare I ask what you are doing?" Dot asked as she marched on the spot, looking at the ground where Julia had been.

"Tying my shoelaces," Julia said quickly, glancing to the cottage and hoping that nobody was looking out of the windows. "Must dash. Need to get back to the café."

Julia kissed her gran on the cheek as she hurried down the road and back to her café. She kept her head down, unsure of who she was hiding from, but feeling like she needed to. It wasn't until she was walking through her café that she noticed her ballerina flats didn't even have laces.

"You took your time," Jessie said as she juggled making an espresso and a cup of tea. "Where have you been?"

"It doesn't matter," Julia whispered, taking over the making of the espresso. "But I think Evelyn is connected to this mess revolving around Barker, I just don't know how."

CHAPTER 9

The morning of Jim's funeral came around quicker than Julia would have liked. She had hoped she would have landed on something vital to crack the case so she could look Jim's family in the eye without being consumed with guilt, but luck had evaded her.

She had kept one eye firmly trained on Evelyn and another on Jeffrey, and despite neither of them appearing to slip up, it had been easier than she had expected to play spy. Evelyn had been visiting her café every day for tea and a scone. At first, Julia had suspected Evelyn had known about her over-the-wall peeking, but if she did know, she was a better actress than Julia had thought. Jeffrey, on the other hand, had been popping up in people's gardens all over the village, no doubt thanks to Dot's glowing recommendation and the juicy titbit about his criminal past. The sound of lawn mowers had been echoing around the village so much, Julia had wondered if she had developed tinnitus on more than one occasion.

She assessed herself in the mirror and attempted to brush Mowgli's cat hairs off her black dress for the fourth time. She picked up her mother's pearls, the only jewellery she had inherited after her death, and held them up to her neck. Squinting, she stepped back, deciding about the jewellery.

"Are you sure you don't want me to come with you?" Jessie asked, appearing in the mirror behind Julia.

"You stay home and enjoy your day off," Julia said as she turned to brush cat hairs off her backside. "You've earned it this week covering for me."

"I don't mind," Jessie said with a shrug as she sat

on the edge of the bed. "I've enjoyed it. If you dropped dead tomorrow, I think I could slip into your shoes, although not those shoes. I don't do heels."

Julia looked down at the black heels, wondering if they were too much. She could hear her sister's voice in the back of her mind telling her they were the only shoes that would go with the dress, even if they did make her calves burn on the few occasions she had worn them.

"Are they inappropriate?" Julia asked as she wobbled on her six-inch stilts. "They're not me, are they?"

"Yes and no," Jessie said, rolling onto the bed to stroke Mowgli, who was curled on top of Julia's pillow. "But who cares? Did you even know the guy?"

"Not really," Julia said. "I knew him as Barker's boss. I only saw him a couple of times, but I want to be there to support Barker. We did find the body as well. I feel like I need to pay my respects to his family."

"Speaking of Barker, he's in the living room."

"How long has he been here?"

"Ten minutes?" Jessie muttered, more interested in Mowgli. "Maybe half an hour."

"Why didn't you tell me?"

"You told me to enjoy my relaxing Sunday."

Julia left Jessie stroking the cat and hurried through to the sitting room, where Barker was fiddling with his tie in the mirror above the fireplace. Julia stepped in front of him and pushed his hands down. She unwrapped the tie and started again, carefully wrapping and looping the fabric. When she was satisfied, she brushed lint off Barker's jacket and kissed him on the cheek.

"I did my father's tie on the morning of my mother's funeral," Julia said as she stood behind him and met his eyes in the mirror. "I was only twelve. That was my first funeral."

"I guess I was lucky. My first one wasn't until I was thirty."

"Somebody close?"

Barker suddenly looked away and started fiddling with his cufflinks. Just when she thought he might answer her question, he walked towards the window and stared up at the sky.

"Looks like it's going to rain," he mumbled.

If it weren't for today's funeral, Julia might have pushed it. It hadn't gone unnoticed to her that his first funeral when he was thirty must have been around the same time as Jeffrey's sentencing. She wondered if this was the tragic event from his past that he had hinted at. He had said it was a story for another day, but it was obvious today wasn't that day.

Julia had attended her fair share of funerals at St. Peter's Church, but never one as busy as Jim Austen's. By the time they arrived, which was still twenty minutes early, the church grounds were fully packed. If Julia had to guess, she would say there were over one hundred people there, a lot of whom were in official police uniform. She had encouraged Barker to wear his uniform, but he had thought it would be insensitive considering his current job status, so he opted for a simple black suit, which he still looked handsome in, but didn't quite feel right for his Chief Inspector's funeral.

When the hearse pulled slowly into the village and circled the green, followed by two black cars, all of the uniformed officers removed their hats and bowed their heads. She spotted Bradley wiping under his eyes with a tissue. She looked to Barker and was surprised when she saw him crying too. She pulled her handkerchief from her bag and discreetly pushed it into his hand.

"Great man," Barker said firmly as he dabbed at

his eyes. "Great man."

Julia looped her fingers through his and squeezed as tightly as she could. He squeezed back to let her know that he appreciated her being there. She had done the same for her father on the day of her mother's funeral in the very same church over two decades ago. Her father hadn't squeezed back.

When the hearse pulled up outside of the church, a group of uniformed men stepped out of the second car and put the coffin on their shoulders. Julia felt a lump rise in her throat when she noticed the police hat on top. A group of weeping mourners got out of the first car, Julia's eyes instantly landing on a grey-haired woman who was sobbing silently into a silk handkerchief. She guessed this was Jim's wife, Pauline, and the young pregnant woman who was comforting her was their daughter, carrying their first grandchild. She looked away, her mind jumping back to that night they had found his body. When she looked back, she was sure she caught the woman scowling in their direction.

The service was a long one, detailing every achievement of Jim's long police career, as well as his large family, and his many hobbies. Julia learned that he had three children, who she could see standing next to their mother at the front of the church. He had started out in the police force as a cleaner and had been inspired to join when he met his wife, who was a constable at the time. He also enjoyed fishing and Italian cooking. It had been easier for Julia to cope not knowing much about the man she had discovered dead, but the reality of the situation was hitting her, and she was even more determined to uncover the truth.

When the priest delivered his final words, the curtains around the coffin closed and John Lennon's '*Imagine*' played through the crackly speakers. Julia and Barker were two of the first to leave the church, having stayed at the back. Julia had told Barker to join his colleagues at the front, but he had insisted on staying where he was.

"Boss," a young constable said to Barker with a nod of her hat. "Good to see you."

"You too, Sarah."

"Shame it's not under better circumstances," she said, taking off her hat and holding it against her chest. "Jim would be proud of the turnout."

"He was a popular man," Barker said. "And a good friend."

"That he was," Sarah said, resting her hand on Barker's arm. "See you at the wake?"

"I don't think so," Barker said with a small

shake of his head. "Not my scene."

"Mine neither, but I think Pauline needs all of the support she can get right now. I'll see you tomorrow."

"Tomorrow?"

Sarah narrowed her eyes and stared at Barker, appearing unsure of what to say. She waited for him to figure out what she was talking about, but when he didn't, she lifted a hand to her mouth and blinked slowly.

"Nobody has told you, have they?" She whispered, looking over her shoulder at her fellow officers as they filed slowly out of the church. "You didn't hear this from me, okay?"

"Hear what?" Barker asked, glancing to Julia, puzzlement evident on his face.

"On the night Jim was murdered he was coming to tell you about your investigatory meeting, which is happening tomorrow. I'm surprised nobody has told you."

Barker gritted his jaw and flared his nostrils as he looked into the faces of his colleagues as they passed him without paying him attention.

"Me too," he replied sternly. "Thank you, Sarah. Your name won't be brought up."

She thanked him with a smile and walked away,

leaving Barker and Julia to retreat to the shade of the large oak tree. Julia tried to think of something reassuring or positive to say, but she knew nothing would make a difference.

"What *is* an investigatory meeting?" Julia asked after a moment's silence.

"It's bad news," Barker said, a shake in his voice. "It means they've reviewed all of the evidence and they want to hear my side of the story."

"Isn't that a good thing?"

"It doesn't usually get to this unless they've found something they don't like," he said, looking darkly into her eyes. "I never thought it would get this far. I've never heard of one of these things going well."

"Surely if you can explain what happened, everything will be okay?"

"I have to plead for my life in front of the Chief Superintendent and whoever has replaced Jim as Chief Inspector, as well as the men in suits from the Independent Police Complaints Commission."

"This is all my fault," she mumbled under her breath. "Barker, I'm so – I'm *so* sorry."

"It's not your fault," he said, cupping her cheek in his palm. "Whatever happens, I'll get through this."

Chocolate Cake and Chaos

"*We'll* get through this," she corrected him.

Barker smiled so genuinely, it warmed Julia to her core, almost making her forget where she was. When she caught that they were being watched out of the corner of her eye, that warmth vanished. She turned to look at Pauline, who was standing alone on the path, her pale eyes red and swollen.

"This is *your* doing," she said, pointing a finger at Barker. "My husband would still be here if it wasn't for *you*."

"Pauline, I'm -,"

"I *don't* want to hear it," she snapped, holding up her hand, which was clinging onto her handkerchief. "Just *go!*"

Her children walked towards her and moved her down the path. Only one of them smiled an apology to Barker, with the others appearing to share their mother's sentiment. Julia turned to Barker, completely stunned by her accusation, but he didn't look as shocked.

"Let's go," he said. "I've done what I came here to do."

Julia nodded and wrapped her hand around Barker's once more. She almost couldn't believe Jim's wife was placing the blame for his death on Barker, and not on the person who had killed him.

It only renewed Julia's urgency to discover the truth.

As they walked out of the church grounds hand-in-hand, Julia spotted Harriet Barnes from Pretty Petals lingering by the gate. When their eyes met, it became apparent to Julia that she was there to see her.

"Julia," Harriet said as she hurried forward while scratching at the pencils holding her messy grey bun together. "I was hoping I would see you here. I put together the flowers for this poor man's funeral, but I hung back to speak to you."

"You did a beautiful job," Julia said with a soft smile, hoping it would serve as a form of apology for their awkward meeting in the florists exactly a week ago.

"Thank you," she said, the sincerity in her voice letting Julia know there was nothing to forgive. "I need to apologise for the way I acted when you came to visit me. I didn't realise the seriousness of the situation."

"It's not you who needs to apologise."

"A man is dead, and I feel like I could have stopped that from happening if I had taken the wreath more seriously. I swear, I thought it was only a prank."

"So did I," Barker said reassuringly. "Don't

blame yourself."

"It's hard not to," she mumbled as she put on her glasses, while pulling a piece of paper out of her pocket. "I tracked down the girl who ordered the wreath. It was entirely by accident. I was shopping in the supermarket out of town, and I spotted her getting into a taxi. I did something idiotic, and I followed her all the way home, to the Fern Moore Estate. Here, I wrote down the address of the flat she went into."

She handed over a scrap of paper to Julia with shaking hands, who read it before immediately giving it to Barker.

"That's Billy Matthews' address," Barker whispered.

"It was a young girl with bright red hair," Harriet said. "That's all I know, I swear. I hope this goes some way to helping, even if it is too late."

"It's not too late," Julia said, resting a hand on Harriet's shoulder. "This is great, thank you."

Harriet smiled her appreciation of Julia's thanks before hurrying off to her small white van, which had her shop's logo printed on its side. Julia made a mental note to make sure to bake that fruitcake for Harriet after all.

"Is she talking about Billy's sister?" Julia asked.

"I saw a girl with red hair in the flat when we visited."

"Mercedes-Mae Matthews," Barker muttered as he closed his fist around the piece of paper. "I should have known."

As they walked towards the lane leading up to her cottage, Julia was already planning the trip she was going to make alone to Fern Moore while Barker was at his investigatory meeting.

CHAPTER 10

In the café the next morning, Julia lined Barker's stomach with a full English breakfast along with multiple cups of coffee, but despite her best efforts to calm him, he was still obviously nervous.

"You'll be fine," Julia reassured him as she topped up his coffee. "Just tell the truth."

"What if the truth isn't good enough?"

"Then at least you've been honest, and you can hold your head high," she said, resting a hand on his shoulder. "Can I get you anything else? A brownie? Or a slice of chocolate cake? I was working on a new version last night with chopped up brownies added into the mix, and I think you're going to really like this one."

"I don't think a chocolate cake will fix this, I'm afraid," Barker said with a sigh before he stood up. "How do I look?"

"Like a man who is going to get his job back," she said as she brushed a piece of white fluff off his shoulder. "You're going to be all right, Barker. I believe in you."

Jessie snorted behind her back, but Julia pretended not to hear. She kissed and hugged Barker one last time and waved him out of the café, watching him walk up to the street until he disappeared from view.

"What are you going to do if he doesn't get his job back?" Jessie asked as she sprayed the front of the cake display cabinet with window cleaner. "You'll have an unemployed boyfriend."

"That's not going to happen."

"But what if it does?"

Julia closed her eyes and tried to smile, wanting

to remain positive so she could be there for Barker, no matter the outcome.

"When you're finished with that, I need you to start on the stock-check," Julia said as she pulled her apron over her head. "I need to ask a girl about a wreath."

"Huh?"

"I'm going to Fern Moore," Julia explained as she pulled on her pale pink peacoat. "I found the address of the girl who ordered Barker's wreath, so that's at least something I can get to the bottom of today. If I figure out whose idea the wreath was, I will be one step closer to discovering the truth."

"You're going to Fern Moore alone?" Jessie asked with a smirk. "You're feeling brave, aren't you? Even I wouldn't go there alone, and I spent six months sleeping on the streets."

"It's not so bad," Julia said, unsure of who she was trying to convince.

"Your funeral."

Julia grabbed her car keys and headed for the door. She remembered what had happened last time she had taken her car to the estate, so she dropped her keys into her bag, pulled out her phone, and called a taxi.

The taxi pulled up in front of the closed play-park, and Julia paid the driver. She was sure he drove away quicker than he would have done if he had been dropping her off anywhere else. She pushed her hands into her pockets and looked up to the flat she remembered as Billy's, the distant sound of a police siren tickling her eardrums. Something rattled behind her, so she spun around, only to see an empty beer can rolling along the street in the breeze.

Knowing it was wise to do what she needed to and leave as quickly as she could, she hurried to the stairwell she remembered taking with Barker and made her way to the second floor.

When she reached it, she hurried along the outdoor walkway. She was sure it seemed scarier than when Barker had been by her side. She looked down at the courtyard, her heart skipping a beat when she didn't spot her comforting Ford Anglia, only to remember the taxi seconds later. In the far corner of the estate, she noticed a large gang of boys heading for the park, cans of beer crammed firmly against their lips. Gulping hard, Julia turned back to the end of the walkway and headed straight for the last flat.

She knocked on the door and waited for Sandra's shrieking voice to yell over the sound of the loud TV. When it didn't, she wondered if she had come all this way only to find that nobody was home. She remembered it was mid-morning on a weekday, and she suddenly felt foolish for expecting to talk to the redheaded teenage girl. Julia turned back to the courtyard and watched as the boys climbed over the fence and into the restricted park. She only spun around again when she heard the chain rattling behind the door.

A flash of red hair and freckled skin caught her attention through the gap, and she felt relieved that her trip hadn't been in vain. She stepped forward, smiling down at the girl, who didn't look much older than thirteen-years-old.

"What?" the girl snapped, her voice quieter than her mother's. "Mum's not in. Come back later."

"I'm here to see *you*, Mercedes," Julia said.

"It's Mercedes-*Mae*."

"Sorry, Mercedes-*Mae*," Julia said, her smile growing. "I wondered if I could ask you a question?"

"No you can't," Mercedes-Mae mumbled, already closing the door. "Go away."

"It's about the wreath," Julia called through the door, turning her ear to the wood. "I'm not going anywhere until you tell me who put you up to that."

Julia stood and listened for almost a minute, but

she heard nothing, other than the TV volume rising. She dropped to her knees and pulled on the letterbox, which was surprisingly loose. She peered into the flat, where she could see the young girl staring at the TV, a baby in her lap. The flat was scarcely decorated and looked in need of a good tidy up.

"I can tell the police what I know," Julia called into the flat. "I'm not sure they'll be as understanding as me."

"You are the police," she cried back without looking away from the TV. "Mum said I'm not to talk to the pigs."

"I'm not the police. I'm a baker. I own a café."

Mercedes-Mae turned and looked at Julia through the tiny slot in the door, her red eyebrows pinching curiously. Julia smiled once more, forgetting her hidden mouth. She wished she had brought one of her cakes to illustrate the fact. She was almost surprised she hadn't thought of that, seeing as her cakes seem to have many uses when it came to discovering information.

To her surprise, Mercedes-Mae put the white haired toddler on the floor and walked over to the door. The chain rattled and the thin door opened before Julia could get up to her feet. Mercedes-Mae walked back into the flat and resumed her seat in front of the large flat screen TV. Julia took the invitation and welcomed herself in, closing the door behind her.

The flat smelled of stale cigarettes and spilt beer. Julia tried not to be too judgemental of the girl's home, which she seemed comfortable in, but she couldn't help but feel like she wanted to start cleaning.

"Can I sit down?" Julia asked.

"Free country."

Julia took that as a yes and sat next to the girl. The toddler, who she realised was a boy, looked up at her as he crammed the corner of the remote control into his mouth. He frowned a little, wary of the stranger in his house.

"You know why I'm here, don't you?" Julia asked politely over the racket of the TV. "To ask about the wreath?"

"I'm not telling you anything," the girl said. "I got fifty quid out of it."

"A man has died."

"I guessed," she said, arching a brow. "That's what wreaths are for, ain't they?"

"A man died *after* the wreath was delivered. *Murdered.* The wreath appeared to be a warning."

Mercedes-Mae turned to Julia, her eyes distrusting. Julia wasn't sure if she seemed truthful to the girl, even though she had nothing to gain from lying to her. She guessed the girl wasn't trusting of many people.

"Why aren't you at school?" Julia asked, deciding to take a different approach.

"Didn't wanna go."

"Why not?"

"Don't like it."

"Doesn't your mother mind?"

Mercedes-Mae shrugged, letting Julia know that her mother didn't care either way. Her heart twitched, but she tried to stay as detached as she could. She reminded herself why she was there and shifted in her seat.

"Don't your friends miss you?"

"Don't got any," she said bluntly. "*Leo*, get off that!"

She snatched the remote control from the baby on the floor, who automatically started howling at the top of his lungs. Instead of comforting her brother, the girl just cranked the TV volume up even more, to the point where Julia could feel the vibrations rattling through the couch and into her body. For a moment, she just sat and observed the situation, but she couldn't just sit there and watch the poor baby cry. Reaching out, she scooped him up and sat him on her knee. He immediately stopped crying and stared at her with his bright blue eyes.

"Hello, Leo," she whispered. "Are you going to be a good boy?"

"He can't understand you," Mercedes-Mae snapped. "He's a baby."

Julia bit her tongue through a smile, wondering how a thirteen-year-old girl could already be so jaded. At her age, Julia had lived a year without her mother, and even she had been more opportunistic and hopeful about life.

"The wreath," Julia continued. "Are you going to tell me who paid you to order it?"

"Some guy," she said casually, her eyes glued to the TV. "I dunno who he was. Came 'round to the estate, gave me the note and fifty quid, and told me where to drop it off. Easy. Got myself these new kicks."

She lifted her feet up, and Julia realised her '*new kicks*' were a pair of brand new pink and yellow trainers, from a brand she recognised on the high street as being from the expensive side. She wondered if the girl's mother even questioned how she had obtained the new shoes, or if she had even noticed.

"What did the man look like?" Julia asked, feeling like she was on the edge of a discovery.

"How am I supposed to know, lady?" she cried, turning the TV up even more as she squinted at the screen. "Had a funny ear."

"Funny ear?" Julia asked, her heart fluttering. "And tattoos?"

"So you already know him?" she asked suspiciously, suddenly turning the TV off. "Is this a trap? Are you the police? I'm calling my brother."

"It's not a trap," Julia said, trying to contain her nerves behind a smile. "Thank you. You've told me everything I need to know."

Julia kissed Leo on the top of his soft, white hair before passing him over to Mercedes-Mae, who reluctantly took him, before dumping him on the floor again. Julia showed herself out, immediately hearing the chain being locked the second she closed the door behind her.

Feeling like a bundle of nervous energy, Julia forgot her earlier fear and pulled her phone out of her handbag and called for a taxi. She waited by the park, scanning the faces of the young boys as they all stared suspiciously at her, some of them throwing insults that landed on deaf ears. At that moment, Julia could take all of the insults in the world because she felt like she had finally made a breakthrough, and that was all that mattered. She searched for Billy's face in the crowd, but she wasn't surprised when she didn't see him. She suspected he would be at the B&B, which was where Julia told the taxi driver to take her.

When the taxi pulled up outside the B&B, she paid the driver and jumped out. She unhooked the gate and ran down the garden path, only stopping when her hand hovered over the chain doorbell. She took a step back and glanced back at the police station, remembering that it was her habit of running into situations before informing the police that had gotten Barker into the exact situation he was in. Just imagining him in the station, tugging at his collar as he tried to explain why he had let a civilian dictate a murder investigation was enough to make her think twice. She doubled back down the garden path, turning once more to the B&B before opening the gate again.

A shiver of panic rattled down her spine when she saw Billy standing in the living room window, his phone to his ear and his eyes trained on her in the shadow of his cap. She began to shake and fear tore through her insides when she noticed Jeffrey standing behind him, his hand resting on Billy's shoulder.

It took all of Julia's energy to turn and unclip the gate. Across the road, she spotted Evelyn climbing off the bus with hands full of shopping bags. Evelyn smiled at her, but Julia couldn't return it. Feeling pale and sick, she dropped her head and headed straight to the police station to tell them what she now knew.

CHAPTER 11

J ulia could remember precise moments in her life when she had felt like her body wasn't her own. The first time she remembered that happening was when she was a twelve-year-old girl, walking through the school corridors after being told her mother's cancer had won. Another time was when she had walked through the streets of London, clutching all of her possessions in four black bags after her husband had changed the locks and left her a note informing her that their marriage was over. As Julia walked towards the desk in Peridale's police station, she knew she was having one of those moments.

"Can I help you, love?" asked the kindly desk sergeant. "You look as white as a ghost."

Julia heard the words, but all she could do was stare. She could still feel Billy and Jeffrey's eyes trained on her through the walls.

"Barker," was all she could say.

As though fate was shining down on her at that moment, Barker walked through a door, tugging off his tie. He looked as beaten down as Julia felt. When their eyes met, she felt her mind return to her body.

"They haven't come to a decision," Barker said with a defeated smile. "They're going to review everything I told them and get back to me. You should have heard the way they were talking to me. It was like I was a criminal, and the new Chief Inspector is a total -,"

"I know who sent the wreath," Julia blurted out. "I went to Fern Moore and spoke to the girl Harriet told us about, Billy's sister."

"You went without me?"

"That doesn't matter," Julia said, waving a hand

dismissively. "I didn't need you charging in doing your Detective Inspector routine, no offence."

The door opened behind Barker, and a group of uniformed officers walked through, laughing at a joke one of them had just told. Barker grabbed Julia and pulled her to the side and out of earshot.

"Well?" he asked, his eyes wide. "Who was it?"

"Oh, Barker," Julia whispered. "She said a man with a *'funny ear'* paid her to place the order."

It took Barker a moment to piece things together, but when he realised whom the man with the funny ear was, his eyes widened, and he looked around the station, his face suddenly pale. It was obvious to Julia that he was experiencing the same out-of-body experience she had only just shaken off.

"Jeffrey," he whispered. "*Jeffrey* killed Jim."

"It gets worse."

"How can this get worse?"

"Billy is in on it somehow." Julia couldn't believe the words that were leaving her mouth, and by the looks of it, neither could Barker. "And I think Evelyn is involved too."

"*Evelyn*?" Barker muttered, almost laughing. "The crazy tarot lady? What have I ever done to her?"

"I don't know, but they're all over at the B&B

right now, and I think they know that I know."

Barker ran his hands down his face as he looked around the station where he no longer held authority. They both looked at the desk, and then to each other, seeming to both realise they had no concrete evidence, aside from a thirteen-year-old girl's testimonial, which she likely wouldn't repeat in the presence of an actual officer of the law.

"What are we waiting for?" Barker asked. "Let's go and finish this once and for all."

"Are you sure?" Julia asked, glancing to the door, still unable to shake off their piercing eyes. "This is what got you into trouble in the first place."

"I need to hear it from his lips, Julia," he whispered, resting a hand heavily on her shoulder. "That man has been haunting me long before he came to Peridale. Besides, we're not going alone."

Barker reached into the inside pocket of his jacket and pulled out his mobile phone. He scrolled through his contacts, hitting the most recent one before pushing it to his ear. With a hand firmly planted on his hip, he looked around the station as he willed the person on the other end to pick up.

"DS Forbes? Bradley? It's Barker. Where are you?"

"Right here."

Julia was surprised to hear the answer come from behind her. They both turned to see Bradley holding open the door of the station with his foot as he bit into a bagel, the phone balanced between his shoulder and ear. A blob of cream cheese fell from the rim of the bagel and down his shirt, but he didn't seem to notice. Julia and Barker both looked to each other, sharing the same grin.

"We know who sent the wreath," Barker said as he pulled Bradley out of the station and into the car park. "It was Jeffrey Taylor."

"The ex-con?" Bradley mumbled through a mouthful of the bagel, as he looked to the B&B. "Are you sure?"

"I tracked down the girl who ordered the wreath," Julia repeated, feeling like time was suddenly running out. "She gave me a description of Jeffrey, mainly his '*funny ear*'."

"He's missing half an ear," Bradley said with a nod, his hand drifting up to his left ear, leaving behind a trace of cream cheese. "If he sent the wreath, he must have killed Jim too?"

"A leopard doesn't change its spots," Barker said, glancing to the B&B. "He's across the road right now. It's your call, DS Forbes."

Bradley finished his bagel and tossed the

wrapper to the ground. He turned from the station door to the B&B, his plump cheeks turning a painful shade of maroon.

"Let's go and see if we can make him confess," Bradley said as he wiped his fingers down the front of his white shirt. "That's what a real Inspector would do, isn't that right, boss?"

"I'm proud of you," Barker said, slapping Bradley on the shoulders. "They'll make a DI out of you yet."

Bradley led the way across the street, a grin spreading from ear-to-ear. He unclipped the gate and scurried down the path to the front door. Julia was pleased to see a pair of handcuffs attached to his belt, but she wasn't sure just one pair would be enough. Bradley looked around for the doorbell, ignoring the sign on the wall instructing visitors to yank on the chain. He opted for knocking on the door. Julia reached around him and pulled on the chain, pointing out the sign to him. He nodded appreciatively.

As they waited for the door to open, Julia could sense Barker's apprehension. She felt she was at an advantage having come face to face with Jeffrey on more than one occasion, but Barker hadn't been so lucky. Despite his face popping up in every garden around Peridale, they hadn't managed to cross each other's paths. Julia did not know if that was purposeful or not.

Through the frosted stained glass panel in the door, Julia saw Evelyn float down the hallway in one of her caftans. She paused halfway and turned to adjust her turban in the mirror. If Julia didn't know better, she would have said the B&B owner was stalling. When the door opened, the smile plastered on her face came across as being obviously false. She didn't look surprised, or shocked to see the three of them there.

"Julia," she cooed, her eyes wide and bright. "Brought me some more of those delicious scones?"

"Drop the act, Evelyn," Bradley said firmly, as though he had just wandered off the set of a 1970s police television show. "Where's Jeffrey? We know he's here."

To Julia's surprise, Bradley's faux-forcefulness cracked Evelyn's façade in seconds. Every muscle in her body seemed to soften as her face dropped. Julia was surprised she didn't press the back of her hand against her turban and faint into a ball on her cream carpet.

"I foresaw this day would come," she mumbled, her face turning a fresh shade of green. "You better come in. Do you mind taking off your shoes? I've just shampooed the carpets."

The unlikely trio kicked off their shoes at the door as they sent unsure glances to each other. Julia hadn't expected a Wild West-style shootout, or for Evelyn to make a run for it, but she hadn't expected a defeated invitation inside. From the curious expression on Barker's face, it appeared he hadn't either. Bradley, on the other hand, looked suspiciously around the hallway as though every trinket and ornament were a crucial piece of evidence.

"Can I get you some Moroccan tea?" she offered as she floated into her sitting room. "I have the most beautiful tea set that I picked up in a souk in -,"

"We didn't come for tea, Evelyn," Bradley said, cutting her off midsentence. "Where's Jeffrey?"

Almost fulfilling Julia's expectations, Evelyn collapsed dramatically into her stylish sofa. She rested the back of her hand against her cheek as she stared off dramatically into the corner of the room. Bradley turned and joined her in staring into the corner as though expecting Jeffrey to mystically appear. Julia arched a brow at Barker, but he sent her a look that read as *'give him a chance'*. Julia almost regretted involving the police on this one occasion. She knew she could get to the point quicker and more successfully, which was why she had gone alone to Fern Moore. She knew her unassuming café-owner exterior was a lot less threatening than two men in suits.

"Before you arrest me, I need you to know why I did it," Evelyn said calmly as she sat up and adjusted the position of her caftan. "I need *my* story to be heard first."

Bradley sat opposite her and pulled a notepad from his pocket. He licked the end of a pencil, flicked to a fresh page, and stared expectantly at her. Julia held in a frustrated sigh. She could almost hear Jeffrey and Billy laughing all the way out of Peridale as they stood there and played along with Evelyn's performance.

"Start at the beginning," Bradley said, his pencil hovering over the paper. "Tell me everything you know."

"I started writing to Jeffrey in prison a year ago," Evelyn said, the creases in her caftan consuming her attention. "I was meditating one day at the bottom of my garden when I heard a call to help those in need. When I came back into the house, one of the guests had left a newspaper open on an article about a program for prisoners who didn't get visitors. It broke my heart. Imagine being locked up like that and not having somebody to talk with? It was *fate*! A sign from the divine creator to help those society had turned its back on. I visited many men and women before I met Jeffrey. I would listen to their stories, and in return, they would listen to tales of my travels. People assume I can't be lonely because I trot around the globe and always have a home full of guests, but sometimes you find the most isolated people in the busiest crowds."

"Was this a – *erm* – sexual relationship between you and Mr. Taylor?"

"Oh, heavens *no*!" Evelyn exclaimed, laughing at the suggestion. "It was merely mentor and student. When I first met Jeffrey, I was taken by his claims of innocence. Of course, everybody I spoke to claimed to be innocent, but his story resonated with me. I believed him."

"He always was manipulative," Barker muttered under his breath. "Did he tell you how he killed six women? How his DNA was on one of the women, and how they found him at the scene of the last murder?"

"Purely accidental, *Detective Inspector*!" Evelyn suddenly sat up and tilted her head to Barker. "Jeffrey was their drug provider, not their murderer.

The victims were all women of the night, were they not?"

Julia was surprised by Evelyn's blunt tone. She turned to Barker to gauge his reaction. The grit in his jaw and the silence of his tongue confirmed what Evelyn had asked.

"The whole case, headed by you, Mr. Brown, was a mess. The real killer confessed all when new evidence cleared Jeffrey's name!" Evelyn reached out and picked up the wooden box on the coffee table. She pulled back the engraved lid and dragged out a deck of tarot cards, which she started to shuffle in her hands. "I always trusted Jeffrey's honesty. The cards told of his innocence every time I have given him a reading."

"The cards tell you what you want to hear," Barker said, shaking his head and pinching between his eyes. "It's hocus-pocus nonsense."

"I once had a reading that told me I would be a firefighter," Bradley mumbled as he stared off into space. "I suppose they weren't far off."

"We all have many paths," Evelyn said, tapping the top of the deck. "Not all of them come true."

"Sounds like a get out of jail free card to me," Barker mumbled.

"Draw your destiny, Detective Inspector."

Barker looked down at the cards, smirking in disbelief. He looked to Julia for guidance, but all she could do was offer a small shrug. She didn't believe in the cards any more than he did, but she knew that Evelyn believed in them, and that was enough for her. To her surprise, Barker relented and drew a card. He turned it over to show a young man sitting under a tree, his arms crossed and his expression stern. A disembodied arm floating in a cloud next to the boy offered a gold chalice, despite him already having three identical cups in front of him.

"*Four of Cups!*" Evelyn exclaimed, taking the card from Barker. "Just as I suspected. It has many meanings. This card proves you are stubborn, Detective Inspector. You are unable to look out of your world to see new offerings. You think you have all of the facts, therefore you will not accept new information, but you are wrong. Jeffrey is innocent, and you are just too stubborn to see it."

Barker shifted on the spot, his cheeks burning brightly. It seemed as though Evelyn had hit a nerve, sending him into silence. In some ways, Julia understood what Evelyn was trying to say, even if she did think it was a coincidence that Barker would pick that card. She was sure Evelyn could have spun any of the cards to tell a story about Barker and his faults.

"This is all well and good, Evelyn, but what about Jeffrey?" Bradley asked, taking the conversation back to their original reason for being there. "How has he come to be in your B&B?"

"When he told me of his release, I insisted he come here," she said as she slotted the cards neatly back into their box. "He was paid handsomely for his false imprisonment, and I recommended he try and find a place to buy in Peridale."

"You told me he had moved from Hull," Julia said.

"I didn't lie to you, Julia."

"You just didn't tell me the whole truth."

"Technically, not a lie."

"But a deception, all the same," Bradley jumped in. "But I suppose if the courts say he is innocent, who are we to argue?"

"Are we forgetting why we came here?" Barker asked, cocking his head suggestively to Bradley. "The wreath?"

"*Quite right!*" Bradley said, repositioning his pencil over the page. "What is your involvement in the wreath that was left on Barker's doorstep?"

"What wreath?" Evelyn asked, her brows pinching tightly together. "I know nothing of a wreath."

"Cut the act, Evelyn!" Bradley demanded.

Evelyn's face disappeared into her neck as she stared at Bradley, her nostrils flared and her eyes filled with confusion. For the first time since they had entered her B&B, Julia felt this was Evelyn being her true self.

"I saw you sneak Billy in here," Julia said, sitting next to Evelyn and resting a hand on her knee.

"Ah, Billy," Evelyn said, nodding her head. "I suspect he is the reason you are here."

"Well, yes," Julia said.

"Restraining orders are unlawful, in my opinion," Evelyn said with a heavy exhale. "Especially between father and son."

As Evelyn stared down at her fingers in her lap, Julia, Barker, and Bradley all looked to each other. Bradley and Barker both shook their head, before training their eyes on Evelyn.

"Jeffrey Taylor is Billy Matthews' *father*?" Barker asked loudly. "You've got to be kidding me."

"Well, *of course*," Evelyn muttered, looking awkwardly to Julia. "I assume that is why you are here? I facilitated a meeting place for them to breach the restraining order. When I heard Jeffrey's story about how he was being blocked from seeing his son, it touched my heart, especially when I learned the son didn't live far from Peridale. Jeffrey only heard that he had a child days before his false imprisonment, and despite numerous attempts to contact the child's mother, she blocked him at every turn. I was the one who told Billy who his father was, and I brought him here to meet him. It was a beautiful thing. A perfect bond that nobody can explain."

"They do have a lot in common," Barker said faintly.

"Which is why I brought Jeffrey to Peridale," Evelyn said, not picking up on Barker's sarcasm. "It was essential for Jeffrey to build a relationship with his son, even if we had to do it in secret. You never know who is watching. I suppose it wasn't going to last forever."

"Do you realise what you've done?" Barker cried. "You were the catalyst those two criminals needed to cook up a murder plot against me!"

"*Murder?*" Evelyn cried, matching Barker's tone and suddenly standing up. "They are *kind* men, Barker Brown! Sweet, *innocent* people."

"Billy Matthews is *anything* but innocent," Bradley whispered as he struggled to keep up with his note taking. "Please, do continue."

Evelyn appeared to grow to match Barker's height somehow, her eyes trained on his. Julia was sure Evelyn was cooking up some spell that she had picked up on one of her travels. She waited for either of them to talk, but when they didn't, she stood up and stepped between them, pushing Evelyn back down to the sofa.

"The thing is, Evelyn, we have proof," she said, sitting next to her and resting her hand on Evelyn's. "Jeffrey paid a young girl, Billy's sister, to order a wreath to leave on Barker's doorstep. One day later, Chief Inspector Jim Austen turned up dead on that same doorstep, in an act that we suspect was meant for Barker. You must be able to see how suspicious this looks?"

"I didn't murder that man," a voice called from the doorway.

They all turned to see Jeffrey Taylor standing in the door, with his tattoo-covered arms folded casually across his chest. Billy appeared behind him, his nostrils flared, and his arms wide and ready to fight.

"Are you confessing to sending the wreath?" Bradley demanded, jumping up and pocketing his notepad.

"I didn't kill that man," Jeffrey repeated, his eyes

darting to Barker, a wicked smirk prickling the edges of his lips. "I *did* want to scare you though. I think it worked."

Julia noticed Barker's fists clench by his side. She jumped up and looped her fingers around his to stop him from doing something he might later regret. Jeffrey darted his brows up and down, begging Barker to do something, but Julia had her hand firmly gripped around his.

"Jeffrey Taylor, you're under arrest for causing a threat by means of intimidation," Bradley said as he pulled the handcuffs from his belt. "You are also under arrest for the murder of Jim Austen. You do not have to say anything. But, it may harm your defence if you do not mention when questioned something, which you later rely on in court. Anything you do say may be given in evidence. Did you get all of that?"

"Here we go again," Jeffrey said coolly, the smirk growing as he turned around, his hands behind his back ready for cuffing. "Billy, get out of here."

Billy stared into his father's eyes with horror, his head shaking ever so slightly. Jeffrey appeared to nod as Bradley tightened the cuffs around his wrists. Billy turned his attention to Barker. He ran his thumb across his neck before doubling back and heading for the door, which slammed behind him. Julia felt Barker about to run after him, but she tugged him back, remembering what had happened last time they had attempted to chase the teenager through the village.

"This way," Bradley said as he tugged his prisoner towards the door. "Don't try anything funny."

To Julia's surprise, Jeffrey went without question. He didn't protest his innocence, nor did he fight his arrest. His lack of objection and complete silence sent an eerie shiver running through the B&B. Barker followed after him, but Julia hung back and looked down at Evelyn who had sunk into the sofa and was wafting herself with a paddle fan.

"I'll put some Moroccan tea on," Julia said.

"Good idea."

CHAPTER 12

The oven beeped, signalling that the Shepherd's Pie was ready. Julia finished lighting the candles, the flame of the match dancing up to her fingers. She shook the small stick, killing the flame.

"*Alright!*" she called to the oven. "*I'm coming!*"

She took a step back and assessed her beautifully set table. It was perfect for the relaxing evening she had planned out for her and Barker to enjoy after two weeks of madness. She dimmed the lights, then ran through to the kitchen and turned off the alarm. A quick glance at the cat clock above her fridge let her know that Barker was five minutes late.

Using her red and white polka dot oven gloves, she pulled the Shepherd's Pie out of the oven, delighted with how beautifully golden the mashed potato had turned. She rested the dish on her cooling rack, yanked off the gloves, and grabbed the white wine from the fridge. She checked the label, unsure of what she was even looking for. Her sister, Sue, insisted it was the best wine at the supermarket, and that had to be good enough for Julia.

"Hurry up, Barker," she mumbled to herself as she poured the wine into two glasses. "Where are you?"

Mowgli jumped up onto the counter and nudged her. She tickled under his chin, but the Shepherd's Pie appeared to be more interesting. He padded along to it, gave it one quick sniff, before jumping off and sauntering over to his cat biscuits.

Julia took the two wine glasses through to the dining room, where the vanilla-scented candles were already infusing the air with their sweet fragrance. She heard a key rattle in the door and smiled to herself as she realigned the forks.

"Great timing," she called through as she dusted down the front of her dress and tossed her hair over her shoulders. "The Shepherd's Pie has just -,"

Julia's voice trailed off as she walked through to the hallway. She was surprised to see Jessie, and doubly surprised to see Barker draped over her shoulder, blood dripping from his eyebrow, and a bunch of squashed flowers in his hand.

"I know I said I'd stay at Dot's tonight, but I didn't want him walking here on his own," Jessie said apologetically as she slumped Barker onto the couch.

"What happened?" Julia asked, rushing to his side.

"Billy Matthews happened," Barker said. "He followed me to Pretty Petals. I got you these."

Barker held up the flowers. They were barely holding together behind their plastic wrapping, but Julia accepted them all the same. She took them through to the kitchen and put them on the counter next to the Shepherd's Pie, which was suddenly lower down on her list of priorities. She soaked a cloth under the cold tap, grabbed a bag of frozen peas from the freezer, and hurried back into the sitting room.

"It looks worse than it is," Barker said with a small laugh as he danced his finger around the bloody cut running through his eyebrow. "I always wanted a scar there. I'll look quite distinguished, don't you think?"

"He only got one punch in," Jessie said from her position on the arm of the couch. "Barker was lucky I was coming back from the shop when I was. I scared him off."

She flexed her knuckles and Julia gasped when she saw they were just as bloody as Barker's eyebrow. She noticed Julia looking, so she pulled her sleeve over them and shook her head to let Julia know she was fine. When Julia had finished cleaning up Barker's cut, she ran back into the kitchen, rinsed the cloth, then cleaned up Jessie's knuckles. She was relieved to only see small grazes underneath the blood.

"Are you going to the police?" Julia asked, turning her attention back to Barker, who winced as he pressed the bag of peas against his brow.

"There's no point," Barker mumbled through the grimacing. "I can't really blame him. Once again, it's down to me that his father is behind bars. They officially charged Jeffrey with Jim's murder this afternoon."

Chocolate Cake and Chaos

Julia was surprised that Barker didn't seem pleased to be saying that. Even though she had her own doubts about the strangeness of what had happened at the B&B, she couldn't logically pin the murder on anyone else.

"I'll leave you two alone," Jessie said, already pulling up her hood. "Dot will wonder where I am. I only went out to buy some food. She's trying to feed me something called quinoa and I don't trust it. See ya."

When they were alone, Julia sat next to Barker and rested her head on his shoulder. He smiled down at her to tell her he would be fine, but it didn't ease her concerns.

"He's just angry that he's lost his dad," Barker said, almost apologetically for Billy. "That, or -,"

Barker didn't finish his sentence. He pulled the bag away and tossed it onto the table. The cut looked deep, and it looked like it needed stitches. Julia ran into her bathroom and grabbed her first aid kit from under the sink. She pulled out a small row of butterfly stitches and antiseptic spray.

"Or what?" Julia asked as she sprayed Barker's brow.

"*Ow!*" he cried out. "What was that?"

"Or what?" Julia asked again, a small grin

forming on her lips as she carefully applied the stitches around Barker's brow. "Do you need some painkillers?"

"I'll be okay," he said with a shake of his head. "What would I do without you, eh?"

"You'd cope."

"That's just the thing," he said, a soft smile on his lips. "I don't think I would. You've been my rock this last month, Julia. I really mean that."

Julia was touched. She sat next to him, her fingers dancing up into the back of his hair.

"Or what?" she repeated for a third time.

"I just can't help thinking that Jeffrey is going along with all of this too easily," Barker said. "What if he's covering for somebody?"

"Billy?"

"It's the most obvious choice."

"It is," Julia agreed. "It's crossed my mind too."

"Or, he really did do it, and he's just accepting that he's going back to prison."

"Did you believe Evelyn's story about him being innocent?"

"Not one word," Barker exclaimed, shaking his head heavily. "Did you?"

Julia didn't answer immediately. She thought about her response for a moment. Evelyn had sounded pretty convinced, and she had put across a strong argument for his innocence. The fact somebody else had confessed to Jeffrey's original crimes was a major sticking point for her.

"I don't know," she admitted. "Mistakes do happen."

"Let me tell you something about Jeffrey Taylor. He's manipulative. He's got Evelyn wrapped around his little finger. Whoever this new person charged with those murders is, I wouldn't be surprised if Jeffrey had someone stitch them up from inside. That little story Evelyn told about Jeffrey being those women's *'drug provider'* was a load of nonsense. He singlehandedly ruled the underground drug scene in Hull. Getting him off the streets was one of the best things I ever did."

"Even if it wasn't for the right crime?"

"He did it, Julia," Barker said stubbornly. "I know he did. Just like he killed Jim Austen. I slept better than I had in weeks last night knowing that monster was behind bars again. I just don't want the charges to be dropped on another technicality. I want the evidence to be so concrete that he can't wriggle out of it. Bradley is rushing ahead, all excited that he's caught Jim's killer, but if this is going to stick, they're going to need more than a wreath and a tiny clip of CCTV footage putting him in the vague area at the time of the murder. If he gets away with this and he stays in Peridale, he's going to be a ghost from my past that I would rather live without."

Julia walked through to the kitchen and plated up the Shepherd's Pie. On her way back to the sitting room, she blew out the candles in the dining room. Leaving the wine behind, she put a pillow on Barker's knee and balanced the plate on top of it.

"So much for a romantic night," Barker said sarcastically. "This looks delicious."

"It's just something I tossed together."

"Certainly looks better than something I would toss together."

As they tucked into their food, Mowgli strolled into the sitting room and jumped up onto the armchair next to them. He circled the same spot for a couple of seconds before curling into a tight ball and falling straight to sleep.

"Wouldn't you just love to be a cat?" Barker remarked as he cleared his plate. "Napping whenever you please, and only worrying about when the next meal is going to be put down. It's an easier life, isn't it?"

"Who wants an easy life?" Julia asked, pushing

her food around her plate. "It's the struggles that make us stronger."

"I'm going to end this year stronger than ever then."

"You've clearly been through struggles before," Julia said as she put her plate on top of Barker's and pushed it onto the coffee table. "You mentioned there was a story you were saving for another time, and I was wondering when that time was going to come."

"Ah," Barker said firmly, dropping his head. "You don't forget a thing, do you Julia?"

"It's a blessing and a curse," she said, tucking her legs underneath her and hugging a pillow as she turned to Barker. "You don't have to tell me anything you don't want to."

"It's not about *wanting* to tell you," Barker said quietly, turning his head and resting it on the back of the couch so that he was looking into her eyes in the low light. "Some things just aren't easy to talk about."

Julia nodded, knowing exactly what he meant. It hadn't gone unnoticed to her that she still hadn't told Barker about her recent divorce. It wasn't that she didn't want to tell him, she just didn't want the shadow of her past staining their still very fresh relationship. She enjoyed being Julia without the baggage of being a divorcee at thirty-seven.

"I was engaged," Barker said, his eyes suddenly darting down. "Eight years ago. It was around the same time I was working on the Jeffrey Taylor case."

"Oh," Julia said, unsure of what she was expecting to hear. "Did it not work out?"

"She died," Barker said, looking back up into her eyes. "When the trial finished, I was being hailed a hero for putting Jeffrey behind bars. I was on cloud nine. I had always dreamed of being a Detective Inspector, and there I was, living that dream. Do you know how many people crack a serial murder case when they're fresh out of their inspector exams? It rarely happens. The night Jeffrey was sentenced, we all went out to celebrate. Everybody was buying me drinks, and even though I had Jeffrey's threat from earlier that day rattling around my brain, I felt like we had done good work. I've already told you about the doubts I had during the trial, but they all vanished that night. It was over, and I was glad of it. I met Vanessa when I first moved to Hull. She was a constable and we worked together a lot. They warned me about mixing business and pleasure, but we fell in love. It all happened pretty quickly, but it was love. I proposed to her that night and she said yes. I didn't even have a ring. I was drunk, if I'm honest with you, but I didn't regret it in the morning.

"We were only engaged for three days when she died. She was shot. It was a random attack. Some lunatic called the police to his house telling them he wanted to report a burglary, and when he invited them in, he shot them both in cold blood. He had been arrested for drunk driving the month before and they had taken his licence off him. That was his little revenge plan. Pathetic, wasn't it? Just like that, she was gone. The other officer pulled through. I went from a career high to the lowest point of my life.

"I tried to get back to normal, but it was impossible. I couldn't walk around the station, or the town, without seeing her everywhere. I transferred to London, and that's where I stayed until I transferred to Peridale."

Julia wiped the tears from her cheek as quickly as they appeared. She tried to speak, to offer Barker her condolences, but she couldn't say anything. With her tear-soaked hand, she grabbed his and squeezed. He smiled his appreciation, the pain of that time alive in eyes.

"Jeffrey being here brought my past crashing

into the present. It was a shock. It brought everything about the trial, and Vanessa flooding back. I felt like I had put enough distance between then and now, but it was like no time had passed."

"A broken heart never fully heals."

"But the place it breaks can sometimes be the strongest part," Barker said, smiling through his sadness. "You're the first woman I've loved since Vanessa. I dated, but nobody ever stuck. You, however, are my silver lining."

"Why didn't you tell me any of this before?" she asked.

"I didn't want you to think I was weak," he whispered. "I didn't want you to think my love for you was any less real because of my past."

Warmth radiated from Julia's chest and flooded through her body. She thought about telling Barker about her divorce, but it felt so insignificant compared to what had just been shared. Clutching his hand and staring deep into his eyes, she felt like she was starting to see the real Barker, and it only made her love him more.

She tried to think of a way she could put those feelings into words, but she knew she could never do them justice. Instead, she cupped his face in her hands and pulled him into a kiss. He fell on top of her, their foreheads banging together. They giggled through their pressed lips, and Julia knew that Barker's heart was singing just as loudly as hers.

CHAPTER 13

The next day in Julia's café, things started to feel more normal again. Every customer talked about the strange newcomer being charged with Jim's murder, thanks to the 'RELEASED MURDERER STRIKES PERIDALE!' headline on the front page of *The Peridale Post*. After the chaos of the last two weeks, hearing the villagers gossiping again reminded her that she was home.

Chocolate Cake and Chaos

"I'm honestly surprised it took them so long," Emily Burns exclaimed, barely pausing after taking a sip of tea. "He mowed my lawn four days ago! He could have killed *me*!"

"And *me*!" Amy Clark chipped in, mumbling through a mouthful of angel cake. "He pruned my roses. Do you know how sharp those sheers are? I'm surprised he didn't cut my head clean off!"

"He only killed Jim because he thought it was Barker," Jessie mumbled under her breath as she cleared away the tables.

Jessie's tolerance for idle village gossip was a lot lower than Julia's, but she wasn't surprised. It seemed that only Peridale natives really understood how things worked. They would talk about the topic until they had discussed and speculated every minuscule detail, and then something new would come along and the cycle would begin again. Luckily for Julia, her customers didn't know her involvement in the solving of the case so her name was left completely out of the story. It was information she was more than happy to keep to herself because she knew if she corrected anybody on their facts, she would become part of the story, and by the time it worked its way around the village, it would have been changed and chopped so much, it

Agatha Frost

would be a completely fictional version of events by the time it made its way back to her.

When the lunchtime rush was over, Dot marched into the café, in her usual new uniform of neon workout clothes. Today she was wearing luminous pink Lycra leggings, a toxic shade of green tracksuit jacket zipped up to her chin, with a matching sweatband covering her forehead. Today, however, she didn't have the usual steely glare of determination she usually had when she was wearing her uniform. She looked completely rundown.

"Cup of tea when you're ready," Dot mumbled as she collapsed into the chair nearest the counter, sweat dripping down her red face. "What's that brown cake in the display?"

"My latest chocolate cake creation," Julia said. "Want a slice?"

"Contaminants," Dot mumbled like a parrot that had swallowed a fitness dictionary. "*Calories.*"

Julia dropped a teabag into a small teapot. As she filled it up with hot water, she looked at her gran, who was staring at the cake display case like a zombie staring at fresh brains. Her tongue poked out of her mouth and ran along her thin lips. Julia glanced to Jessie, who was also watching. Jessie rolled her eyes and opened the display case, pulling out the large cake.

"Are you sure you don't want some, Dot?" Jessie asked, waving the cake under her nose. "It's Julia's best work yet. A milk chocolate sponge with chocolate fudge buttercream, topped off with flaked chocolate that just melts in your mouth."

"Get it away from me!" she cried, fear rushing across her face.

Jessie rolled her eyes and placed the cake onto the counter. She grabbed the teapot Julia had just made up and positioned it in front of Dot, along with a teacup, a pot of milk, and sugar. Dot added the milk, but ignored her usual three sugar cubes.

"Why won't this thing stop vibrating?" Dot cried, shaking her wrist against her ear. "All night and all day. Beeping and booping at me! Telling me to breathe, and stand, and walk, and measuring my heart rate like a demonic doctor obsessed with my blood pressure."

"Just take it off," Julia offered.

"I *can't*!" Dot said with a shake of her head. "Do you know how much this thing cost? A whole month's pension, that's how much!"

"You're crazy," Jessie whispered. "Absolutely nuts."

Dot lifted the cup of tea to her lips with shaking

fingers, but her eyes were firmly honed in on the chocolate cake. Julia had made the new version that morning to surprise Barker with, but she had decided to put it up for sale in the café first, and she was only taking home the leftovers so that Barker couldn't complain that she was trying to fatten him up.

"Here it goes again!" Dot cried as her watch beeped. "It's telling me to breathe! *I am breathing!* Does it think I'm dead? Tell it to stop, Julia!"

"Leave my gran alone," Julia teased, pointing a finger at the watch. "Or else."

"Do you think this is a joke?" Dot yelled, scratching at her skin under the watch. "It's taken over!"

"Isn't the whole point of a club that you spend time with people you like and do something fun?" Julia asked. "This doesn't look much fun, Gran. You're sitting here on your own shouting at a watch."

"But what about my steps?" Dot cried as she shook the watch against her ear again. "If I don't complete my steps goal, I don't get the little medal on the screen. I haven't missed a day!"

"You know if you shake your arm, it clocks up the steps?" Jessie offered as she walked by.

"But that's pointless."

"It works," she said with a shrug. "You're the sucker who's letting a watch control your life."

Before Dot could launch into an impassioned rant about why the watch was the best thing she had ever bought, the bell above the café rang out, and Shilpa Ahmed from the post office next door walked in.

"Afternoon, all," she said. "We appear to be matching today, Dot."

Shilpa motioned to her green sari, which was a similar shade of green as Dot's sweatband, but somehow looked much more delicate with its embroidered white floral pattern and flowing design. Dot didn't seem to take the compliment well. She tore off her sweatband, ripped off the watch, and tossed them both to the floor. Using her heel as a weapon, she stomped down on the watch, cracking the screen. As a final act of defiance, it beeped back at her, causing her to stomp down until she was looking at a pile of grass and microchips.

"*Are you happy now?*" she screamed at the top of her lungs at the mess on the floor. "Will you leave me alone?"

"Is it something I said?" Shilpa whispered to Julia.

Julia shook her head as she cut a large slice of the cake. Before she could stab a fork into it, Dot snatched the cake from the plate with her fingers and crammed it into her mouth. Her eyes rolled back into her head and for the first time since starting her fanatical health kick, she looked peaceful.

"You're free now," Jessie said as she massaged Dot's shoulders. "Congratulations."

"S'good cake," she mumbled through half-closed lids as the sugar surged through her body. "S'good."

Julia chuckled at her gran, glad that she was back. She had always thought her gran's stiff white blouses, held under her chin with a brooch, and pleated calf-length skirts were a little old fashioned, but she was looking forward to getting them back if it meant she never had to see her gran decked out in neon ever again.

"What can I get you, Shilpa?" Julia asked. "I have some of those red velvet cupcakes you like."

"You know how to spoil me," she said as she glanced through the cake display case. "I'll take two. One for now, and one for later."

"Good idea," Dot said wisely, wagging her finger at Shilpa. "I like your style."

Julia reached down to pluck the two cupcakes out of the counter display. As her fingers closed around the first cupcake, something burst through her café's window, sending shattered glass flying through the air. Dot and Shilpa both let out wild screams as a chunk of Cotswold stone rolled across the floor, stopping when it snagged on Dot's sweatband. They all peered through the fresh hole in the window and onto the village green, where Billy Matthews was standing in his red tracksuit, his hands firmly in his pockets.

"I'm gonna kill him!" Jessie yelled as she ran for the door.

Billy set off running but Jessie was hot on his heels. As the pair disappeared from view, Julia pulled her phone from her bag under the counter, her hands shaking out of control. Staring down at her screen, she wondered if she should call the glaziers or the police first.

"Is everybody okay?" Julia asked, looking up from her phone as she dialled '*999*'.

"I'm fine," Dot said as she resumed her cake, which was much more important to her at that moment. "Honestly, that boy is nothing but a menace."

"I'm surprised he's walking around the streets, considering he was one of those three people on that security footage I gave to the police," Shilpa added.

Julia pressed the phone against her ear and listened to the dial tone. Somebody answered, asking what emergency service she wanted, but all she could do was stare at Shilpa, unsure of what she was even supposed to be saying to the operator on the other end.

"Wrong number," Julia mumbled into the handset before tossing it on the counter and looking directly at Shilpa. "Did you say *three* people?"

"Well, yes," she said, almost unsure of herself. "How do you know about that?"

"I was shown the footage. I saw Jeffrey, and I saw Billy."

"And the third person," Shilpa said, nodding surely. "The third person dressed all in white."

Julia's heart stopped. She looked through the broken window, suddenly feeling the world grinding to a halt around her. In her mind's eye, she could see Barker alone, and probably still asleep in bed.

"Do you still have that footage?" Julia asked, already grabbing her coat from the hook in the kitchen.

"Of course," Shilpa said. "We keep all security footage for thirty days. I merely gave the police a copy. Is it important?"

"Very. I think it might just prove who *really*

killed Jim Austen."

Leaving her gran in charge of the café, Julia followed Shilpa into the post office next door. Her son, Haaken, was behind the counter, but when he saw his mum return, he grabbed his coat and headed for the door.

"Don't forget it's your uncle's birthday tonight!" Shilpa called after him. Haaken waved his hand over his head, his headphones already in his ears.

After Shilpa punched in the code to unlock the door, they both walked behind the counter and towards a small computer crammed between a tall filing cabinet and a basket full of parcels.

"Let me see if I can remember how this thing works," she muttered to herself as she hovered over the keys. "It was a Monday, wasn't it?"

"The day after the beer festival."

"Ah, yes," Shilpa said with a nod. "I remember, not that I drink. I think this is it."

Shilpa clicked a file and a video jumped up on screen. She pressed the play button and started fast-forwarding through the clip. Julia watched as the sunny morning turned into the dull afternoon. When the storm clouds appeared and prematurely darkened the village, Shilpa slowed the footage down to normal speed.

Julia saw Billy Matthews, just as she had before. He walked up the lane, staring down at his phone, and only looking up when he was outside of Barker's cottage. She realised the footage she had seen had been cropped so that Barker's cottage had been cut entirely out of view.

"Here's the next one," Shilpa said, tapping her finger on the screen.

Jeffrey Taylor came into shot, running across the village green. He turned onto the lane, only slowing down when he reached Billy. They hugged and then turned in the direction of Barker's cottage. Julia's heart stopped, but to her surprise, they climbed over the wall and disappeared into the fields surrounding their cottages.

Seconds later, a car pulled up outside of Barker's cottage and a man jumped out. He locked the car over his shoulder and walked towards Barker's front door.

"This is when it started raining," Shilpa said just as the rain began to fall. "Gets a little trickier to see, but if you look closely, you can see the white figure."

Julia leaned into the screen, the distance of Barker's cottage already difficult to see without the added difficulty of the rain blurring the footage. Just when she thought she wasn't able to see whatever Shilpa thought she had seen, something large and white stepped out from the side of Barker's cottage.

"I thought it was a ghost," Shilpa whispered. "Creepy, isn't it?"

Julia squinted, her nose practically touching the screen. Through the blurry pixels, she watched the ghostly figure walk to the door, and then suddenly walk away and hop over the same wall Billy and Jeffrey had. She pulled back when she realised she had just witnessed Jim's murder through the blur of the rain. If she hadn't have known what had happened, she would never have been able to tell what she was looking at, but because she had been able to think about nothing else since that dreadful night, something in her brain suddenly clicked and the door blocking her logical mind from truly figuring things out unexpectedly burst open.

"That's not a ghost," Julia whispered, taking a step back from the screen. "It's a forensics suit. I need to go. Thank you, Shilpa."

Before Shilpa could ask her any questions, Julia ran out of the post office, ignoring the small crowd that had formed around her café's broken window. With Barker's life more at stake than ever, shattered glass was the last thing on her mind.

She set off towards Barker's cottage, relieved when she saw DS Forbes out of the corner of her eye drinking a pint outside of the The Plough.

"Julia!" he beamed over his pint, froth in his moustache. "Join me for a pint?"

"It's you who I need to join me, DS Forbes," she said hurriedly. "There's not a lot of time to explain, but we need to get to Barker's cottage right now. His life might be in grave danger and I don't trust anybody else other than you right now."

"Grave danger, you say?" Bradley asked, a brow arching curiously as he stood up. "Lead the way, young lady!"

Thankful that she didn't have to explain herself any more, she set off towards Barker's cottage with Bradley hot on her heels.

CHAPTER 14

Bradley banged on the door, calling out for Barker through the wood. They both listened, but they couldn't hear a thing. Julia stepped over Barker's weed-infested flowerbed, and then cupped her hands up against the sitting room window.

"I can't see him," Julia whispered.

"Maybe he's not home?"

"Or maybe we're too late." Julia climbed back over the flowerbed and dove into the hanging basket next to the door, her fingers closing around something cold and metal. "For emergencies."

She shook the dirt off the key and crammed it into the lock. To her relief, the door opened with ease. They both looked at each other before stepping into the dark cottage.

"Barker?" Bradley called out. "You home?"

"I'll check the bathroom," she said. "He sometimes likes to take bubble baths with the radio on. You look in the bedroom."

"Gotcha."

When they had both finished checking the rooms, they met in the hallway, neither of them having found Barker. Julia pushed her fingers up into her hair and turned on the spot.

"Why do you think he's in danger?" Bradley asked.

"Somebody tried to kill him, and it wasn't Jeffrey," Julia said as she pulled her phone from her handbag. "Jeffrey might have left the wreath, but he didn't commit murder. I'm going to try and call Barker."

Julia tapped a couple of buttons on her screen and put the phone to her ear. She waited a moment before tossing the phone down onto the side table.

"He's not picking up," she said as she clipped her handbag shut. "Maybe we should just wait for him to get back?"

"How do you know Jeffrey isn't the murderer?" Bradley asked, looking as confused as ever. "We charged him yesterday morning."

"Has he confessed?"

"Well, no, but murderers don't tend to when they don't want to go back to prison."

"I have proof Jeffrey didn't kill Jim. Somebody tampered with Shilpa's security footage, cutting out a crucial piece of evidence. In its entirety, it proves Jeffrey and Billy's innocence. Why did you crop yourself out of the video, DS Forbes?"

Silence fell on the cottage, perhaps the whole village, and Julia was sure she could hear a pin drop. She dropped her smile, tilted her head forward and stared at Bradley from under her brows.

"*Excuse me?*" he spluttered, forcing a laugh through his reddening face. "Are you insinuating that *I* tampered with evidence?"

"I'm implying that you *murdered* Jim Austen and you went to great lengths to conceal your tracks." Julia's heart pounded as she glanced down at the phone. She felt every detail of the last two weeks flooding to the forefront of her mind. She couldn't believe it had taken her so long to figure it out. "You never wanted to kill Jim, did you, DS Forbes? Your tears at his funeral were real, but they weren't tears of grief, they were tears of guilt."

Bradley's expression darkened as he glared at Julia, the air around them turning cold as gloomy clouds rolled over Peridale, casting out the little afternoon daylight that was reaching them in Barker's hallway. With his back to the front door, dark shadows cast down Bradley's face, his plump cheeks forcing his eyes deep into his skull.

"Why would I kill Jim Austen?" he mumbled, droplets of sweat forming on his brow. "He was the best Chief Inspector this town has seen."

"Because you thought he was Barker," she said, the veins in her temples throbbing. "All of your little comments about taking Barker's job and becoming a DI weren't jokes, were they? You wanted his job so badly that you would kill for it. Barker told me people in the station resented him for moving into the village and filling the position. You might not have been vocal about it, but you resented him more than most."

"I've worked my backside off in that station!" Bradley cried, spit flying from his mouth as his usually squeaky voice deepened. "I have given them forty-one years of my life! I've worked in that station since I was eighteen-years-old and I've been held back at *every* turn! Every man in my family for generations has been an inspector, and they've kept me stuck as a sergeant doing the grunt work. Do you know how *embarrassing* that is for me? I thought I was getting that job! I figured it was finally *my* time to go through my inspector's exams and prove everybody wrong! I retire in seven years. I'm running out of time! I have to go home and look my wife in the eyes every day and tell her '*not today, but maybe tomorrow*'. I thought my tomorrow had come, and then Barker Brown moved to the village and snatched *my* chance from under my nose!"

"It's not Barker's fault you didn't get promoted."

"But Barker is so perfect!" Bradley cried as he started to pace from side to side. "He's handsome, slender, has a full head of hair, a beautiful girlfriend, a lovely home, a great salary, and he's twenty years younger than me! I've put in *my* work. What has *he* done to get here? He's coasted through! His suspension was *my* time to shine! It was *my* day!"

"Why not just wait for the outcome of his investigatory hearing?" Julia asked, squinting into the dark as the clouds thickened. "There was a chance he wasn't even going to keep the job."

"Jim was pushing him through," Bradley sneered through gritted teeth as he slammed his fist into his palm. "Jim was a good man, but he was *blind*. He thought Barker was the fresh breath of air this village needed. *Ha*! What's wrong with the old ways? What's wrong with helping out your own? Before Jim came here that night, he told me he was coming to let Barker know about his hearing, and that he was going to try his best to get Barker his job back. *Why*? *He* didn't deserve it! *I* deserved it."

"So you thought you would stop Barker before he even had a chance to hear what Jim had to say?"

"The timing was just too perfect!" Bradley cried, a sinister laugh forcing its way through his lips. "Do you know who the most successful criminals of all time are? The ones who strike when the timing is *right*! The wreath was *too* perfect. Murder had never even crossed my mind until then, but it was an opportunity I had to take!"

"So you took a forensics suit and waited behind his cottage for him to come home," Julia offered. "You know better than anyone how easy it is to leave behind trace evidence. You waited for Barker, and you hit him with a rock from his garden, except it wasn't Barker."

"It was dark!" he snapped, suddenly standing still and pointing a finger in Julia's face. "People always used to say they looked the same from behind. I never saw it until -,"

"Until you saw Jim's face."

"I tried to save him," he cried, his voice cracking. "He was dead in seconds."

"You took his wallet and phone to make it look like a mugging gone wrong, and you dumped them somewhere obvious so somebody would find them and strengthen your plan."

"Billy finding the phone was a stroke of pure luck! I knew I could get away with it. When Shilpa handed me that security footage, I thought I had been caught. Turns out she didn't know what she was looking at. Who knew cropping a video could be done on a phone? I never even submitted that evidence, but I knew you were sticking your nose in, so I showed it to you so you would push yourself towards Jeffrey and Billy. I knew *you* of all people wouldn't be able to keep your nose out, and if anybody was going to help me frame them, it was Julia South, baker extraordinaire!"

"And it almost worked," Julia agreed with a nod. "Everything I found did lead me to Jeffrey and Billy, except one thing."

"What's that?"

"My gut instinct," Julia said, taking a step towards the man in the dark. "I assumed Jeffrey was guilty because I wanted to believe Barker was safe with him out of the picture, but something didn't sit right with me. Looking back now, it's so obvious. You couldn't help but keep slipping in how much you wanted to be an inspector. Your ego let you down."

Bradley continued to pace back and forth, his eyes trained on the ground. He darted his fingers up to his head and rubbed the bald patch, disrupting the faint strands of hair that remained. He mumbled to himself, nodding his head and laughing sinisterly under his breath.

"Too bad nobody will believe you," Bradley said as he tapped his finger on his chin. "You've already caused enough trouble. Nobody is going to take the word of a baker over a Detective Sergeant, and soon to be inspector! There's no way Barker is getting his job back now, and after I arrested Jeffrey, they have to let me take the exams."

"And you'll let an innocent man spend the rest of his life in prison for a crime he didn't commit?"

"He's done it once!" Bradley cried. "What's

another life sentence? He has no life here. He's going to rot behind bars, and I'm going to get away with this! It's the *perfect* crime!"

"Maybe nobody will believe *me*," Julia said as she stepped forward to pick up her phone. "But maybe they will believe *you*. I recorded this entire conversation. I knew Barker wasn't here. He's not been back here since the murder. He's asleep in my cottage as we speak, I just knew I needed to let you think I trusted you. The thing is, DS Forbes, men like you are so desperate to be acknowledged that you'll confess to a crime because you think you got away with it so well. Maybe you should have listened to your *own* gut?"

Bradley's nostrils flared, and his cheeks burned the deepest shade of maroon she had seen as he stared down at his protruding stomach. Just at that moment, the heavens opened, and rain pelted down on the cottage's roof, echoing around the corners of the dark hallway. The open door rattled in its frame, the hinges screeching out for oil. They watched each other through the dim light like two alley cats waiting for the other to make the first move. A bolt of purple lightning cracked through the sky, illuminating the handcuffs strapped to his belt.

"You know I can't let you leave?" Bradley

whispered as he took a step forward, his hand reaching out for the phone. "You should have just stuck to your baking. I'm going to miss your lemon drizzle cake."

Julia looked down at her phone, and then down to the handcuffs. A gust of wind forced the door open, startling both of them. It bounced into the room and back into its frame, the small glass panel shattering in an instant. They both looked at it for a second, but nothing was going to stop Bradley. He turned back to Julia, fury filling his beady eyes.

He took his moment and dove forward, his fingers grazing against the edge of the phone. Julia darted to the side and with all of her force, she pushed the round man towards the hallway side table. He tried to catch his balance, but he was too heavy and gravity was too strong. He reached out for air as he stumbled backwards into the radiator before crashing down onto the small oak table, which buckled under the weight. Julia dropped the phone and struck, ripping the handcuffs from his belt. She wrapped one end around his chunky wrist and the other to the radiator pipe. At the moment he realised what was happening, she jumped back and watched as he struggled to stand.

"You're going to pay for this!" he cried as he

rattled his hand against the pipe.

Another crack of lightning flashed through the hallway, its purple hue catching the glass screen of her phone, which was still recording every word. They both spotted it at the same time, but Julia's hands closed around it first. As she attempted to move away, Bradley reached out and wrapped his fingers around her brown curls and yanked her head back. Burning pain soared through her scalp, and she was sure he was about to rip her hair right out. She yelled out in agony, but the rumbling thunder drowned her.

Julia cried out for help, but she knew it was in vain. He wrapped her hair around his fist and yanked even harder as he tried to grab the phone with his cuffed hand. She reached up to her head and tried to pull his fingers away, but they were fused so tightly, she wasn't going to be able to do it with one hand. Despite this, she didn't let go of the phone.

"Let go!" he yelled as he jerked her hair. "Let go right *now!*"

Another bolt of lightning cracked through the sky and the pressure around her hair released. She paused for a moment, unsure of what was happening. When she realised he had let go, she scrambled to the bathroom door and out of his reach, clutching the phone in both hands.

Through her tears, she saw Bradley slump against the radiator. What she first thought was an unfortunate well-timed bolt of lightning striking the cottage and travelling through the pipes revealed itself to be a hooded figure standing in the doorway.

"I think I've split my knuckles this time," she heard Jessie say.

Julia wiped her tears away and let herself breathe. She looked down at the blurry phone screen and finally ended the recording. She saved a copy to her phone and sent it to Barker, just to be safe.

"Your timing is impeccable as ever," Julia whispered as Jessie helped her up off the ground.

"I was heading back to the cottage to find you. I managed to catch Billy, and they arrested him for smashing your window. I saw Barker's open door, so I thought I'd be a good neighbour and close it, but of course, you're here, and there's a fat man handcuffed to the radiator. Do I want to know where this was going?"

They both looked down at Bradley as he rolled his head around his shoulders, letting out a deep groan as his face clenched up. Julia wrapped her arm around Jessie's shoulder and pulled her into a hug.

Chocolate Cake and Chaos

For the first time since the appearance of the wreath, she relaxed, and all she could do was force out a relieved laugh.

CHAPTER 15

The rain continued through the night, but the sun rose brighter than ever in the morning, pushing every last cloud out of the sky to reveal nothing but crystal blue clearness for miles in every direction. Julia woke refreshed knowing that Barker was safe once more. Sitting up in bed with the sheets wrapped around her, she looked down on him and smiled. One of the butterfly stitches on his brow had popped up during the night, so she gently pressed it back down.

"It's weird to watch people when they're asleep," he mumbled through the side of his mouth, his eyes still closed. "I was having the strangest dream."

"Was it about me making you breakfast in bed?"

"No, it was about Bradley. I still can't believe I thought we were friends. It's already slipped away now, but I'm sure he was trying to kill me – *again*."

Julia pulled on her pale pink robe and walked through to the kitchen, feeling light without the weight of an unsolved murder on her shoulders. Her heart still ached for Jim, but it brought her some comfort knowing his family now knew the truth. She hoped they would find it in their hearts not to blame Barker for Bradley's illogical actions.

After feeding Mowgli, Julia set out three plates and got to work making breakfast. When she finished, she placed the fried eggs, sausages, bacon, baked beans, toast, and black pudding on the plates. She put two of them on one tray, and the third on another.

"It's just me," Julia whispered through Jessie's door as she knocked softly. "I've made breakfast."

Julia pushed the door, and it opened with ease. Jessie was already sitting up and at her dressing table, staring into the mirror with something silver pressed against her lips. She dropped whatever was in her hand and looked down. Julia met her eyes in the mirror, and she was surprised to see Jessie playing with her lipstick.

"Looks better on you than me," she said as she placed the tray on the edge of the bed. "You can keep it."

"Doesn't matter," Jessie said as she wiped the subtle berry shade off her lips with the back of her hand. "Looks stupid."

"You're fine just the way you are," Julia said with a small wink. "You don't have to wear makeup to impress anyone."

"Who said I was trying to impress someone?" she snapped, looking down her nose at Julia through the reflection, the berry stain smudged across her chin.

Julia kissed Jessie on the top of the head and backed out of the room, leaving her to her breakfast. She picked up the second tray and walked through to the bedroom, where Barker was sat up in bed, his phone pressed against his ear, and a smile firmly on his lips.

"Thank you very much, sir," Barker said with a nod. "I'll be in later today. Again, I can't thank you enough. I'll see you soon."

Julia placed the tray in between them and crawled up the bed and back under the covers. She scooped up some of the beans with her toast and crammed it into her mouth.

"Who was that?" Julia mumbled through her food.

"That was my new Chief Inspector," Barker said as he tapped his phone against his palm with a smile. "He just wanted to let me know that in light of recent events, they're dropping their investigation into my conduct and reinstating me with immediate effect."

"Barker, that's amazing!" Julia beamed, wiping baked bean sauce off her chin as it drizzled from the toast. "I'm so proud of you."

"It was all you, Julia," he said. "You're a better DI than I'll ever be, even if I am the best detective in the country when you compare me to a crazed killer desperate for a promotion."

"Perhaps," Julia said with a nod as she mopped the toast around the beans. "But I promise I will leave all detective inspecting to you from now on."

"Why does that sound like a lie?"

Julia's cheeks blushed as she dunked the crust of her toast into the runny egg yolk before tossing it into her mouth. She occupied herself with eating until Barker did the same, and she was glad when he didn't push her to admit she might have stretched the truth a little. She decided she wouldn't actively go searching for any more murderers unless she needed to. With Barker back where he belonged, she was confident that Peridale was in safe hands once more.

After breakfast, they all walked down to the café, where Julia was surprised to see Dot organising two men as they fitted a new pane of glass in her café's empty window frame.

"Gran!" Julia cried. "You did all of this?"

"It's the least I could do, love," she said, without taking her eyes away from the glaziers. "Little higher on the left there boys."

Both of the men looked at each other, and it was apparent to Julia that Dot had been bossing them around since they had arrived. She turned to the village green and inhaled the fresh spring air, glad of the normalcy once more. She knew the moment her café opened, all people would want to talk about was Bradley Forbes' arrest, but if it was any other way, it wouldn't feel like home. It would only be a matter of time before something else occupied the gossipers' attention.

"Here comes trouble," Barker whispered into Julia's ear as he nodded up the road. "Maybe I should go."

Julia looked towards Evelyn's B&B to see Jeffrey and Billy walking side by side towards them. Julia wrapped her fingers around Barker's hand to let him know that she was there. It was inevitable that they would bump into each other eventually. In Julia's eyes, the sooner they got it out of the way, the better.

Jeffrey and Billy whispered back and forth as they approached. Julia prepared herself for an all out war, and she could feel Jessie doing the same. Her fists clenched tightly by her side, so Julia did what she had done to Barker, and she held her hand. With Barker and Jessie with her, Julia held her head held high as Jeffrey and Billy walked up to them, stopping only inches away.

With his head cocked back, Jeffrey stared down at Barker, his lips tight and his jaw tense. Julia expected Jeffrey to try and plant a fist on the end of Barker's nose, so she was more than surprised when he outstretched a hand.

"Truce," Jeffrey said calmly. "There's no point going around in circles."

Barker looked to Julia and then down at the

hand. She was worried he would be stubborn and refuse to take it, but to her relief, he slapped his hand into Jeffrey's, and they shook firmly. A small smirk, kinder than the one she had previously seen from him, tickled Jeffrey's lips. She looked down at his hand as he let go of Barker's, noticing that the tattoos on his left knuckles spelt out '*C E N T*'. Combined with his other hand she had seen when she first met him, she realised his knuckles read '*I N N O C E N T*'.

"I'm sorry for the wreath," Jeffrey said as he pushed his hands into his baggy jeans pockets. "I was surprised to see you here. I wanted to scare you, and that was wrong of me."

"Right, yeah," Barker mumbled, clearly taken aback by the apology. "And I'm sorry for everything too."

"Apology accepted," Jeffrey said before nudging Billy firmly in the shoulder. "Is there something you want to say, son?"

Billy sighed and rolled his eyes. He looked down at the ground and circled his white trainers around in the dust. For the first time since encountering the young criminal, Julia saw him as the child that he was.

"Sorry for hitting you," he mumbled to Barker.

"Sorry for smashing your window."

"And the rest," Jeffrey demanded.

"Sorry for trying to nick your bag, but I already apologised for that one."

"Yeah, not good enough," Jessie growled, letting go of Julia's hand. "Truce or no truce, I'll still kick your backside if you try anything again."

"I don't doubt it," Billy said with a small smirk, sending a wink in Jessie's direction.

Jessie blushed and suddenly dropped her dark hair over her face. Julia wondered if this was whom the attempted lipstick application had been for.

"I need to set a better example for my son," Jeffrey said as he slapped his hand down on Billy's shoulder. "It's a fresh start for all of us. You're going to stay out of trouble, aren't you kid? And you're going to pay this lady back for the window."

"Suppose so," Billy mumbled with a shrug.

"Well, I appreciate that," Barker said awkwardly. "Now that I have my job back, I'll hold you to it."

Billy narrowed his eyes on Barker before rolling them and turning around. Jeffrey smiled one last time before spinning on his heels and following his son back towards the B&B. They continued to whisper back and forth until they suddenly stopped outside of The Plough. Billy turned and ran back towards them, and Julia almost thought the truce was over already. Instead of running towards Barker, he ran towards Jessie.

"Call me," he said as he passed a small piece of paper with a phone number scribbled on it to her. "I like a girl who can keep up with me."

Jessie stared down her nose at the piece of paper, seemingly unable to look him in the eyes. Julia almost expected her to screw it up and toss it back at him, but she slyly pocketed it in her hoody.

"Yeah, whatever," she mumbled. "Loser."

Billy shook his head and laughed as he turned and jogged back to his dad. Jeffrey slapped him on the back, and they continued walking up to the B&B, ready for their fresh start. Julia smiled and shielded her eyes from the sun when she saw Evelyn welcoming them inside.

"What now?" Julia asked Barker as they turned back to the café arm in arm with Jessie trailing behind, no doubt looking at the phone number.

"I guess we go back to normal," Barker said, holding the café door open for Julia as the workmen wiped down the fresh pane of glass. "Is there any of that chocolate cake left?"

If you enjoyed *Chocolate Cake and Chaos*, why not sign up to Agatha Frost's **free** newsletter at **AgathaFrost.com** to hear about brand new releases!

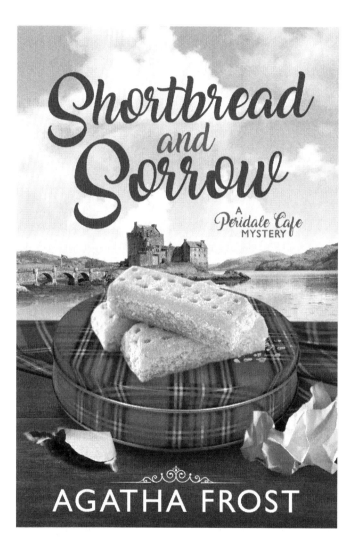

Coming May 2017! Julia and friends are back
for another Peridale Café Mystery case in
Shortbread and Sorrow!

Made in the USA
Lexington, KY
07 August 2019